T0208692

THE
ROCK
CRYSTALS

Asif Saba

authorHOUSE®

AuthorHouse™ UK
1663 Liberty Drive
Bloomington, IN 47403 USA
www.authorhouse.co.uk
Phone: UK TFN: 0800 0148641 (Toll Free inside the UK)
    UK Local: (02) 0369 56322 (+44 20 3695 6322 from outside the UK)

Published by AuthorHouse 11/07/2023

ISBN: 979-8-8230-8530-4 (sc)
ISBN: 979-8-8230-8531-1 (hc)
ISBN: 979-8-8230-8529-8 (e)

Library of Congress Control Number: 2023920555

Print information available on the last page.

This book is printed on acid-free paper.

This is a work of fiction. All of the characters, names, incidents,
organizations, and dialogue in this novel are either the products
of the author's imagination or are used fictitiously.

CONTENTS

DEDICATION

To the reader.

I thank you so much for inviting me into your life.

May you see beyond what is in this book
and then write your own book.
In Sha Allah. (God Willing)

What you believe is impossible will show up in
someone else's awareness as a possibility.

Acknowledgements

I thank Allah for all the inspiration I received during the writing of this book. I give thanks for the guidance that brought me into contact with the following individuals that played a part in the completion of this book.

I thank Paula. She is an amazing editor. She brought the story to life and gave it depth.
Editor and Proofreader – Paula Kench
www.bronteproofedit.co.uk

Cover Design – Jacqueline Abromeit
www.goodcoverdesign.co.uk

To Paul, Sara, Tasneem, Nazish, Mariyah, Earl, Joanne and Dorcas.
To Humair – www.radiomac.org

A Strange Vision

S hut away from the rest of the house, Yusif sat cross-legged on the floor, in quiet meditation, with his eyes closed. This was his second meditation of the day, having already done his morning meditation earlier. In his mind's eye, he watched, a strange image appeared. He had seen parts of this vision previously, however, this version seemed fuller, more detailed and more complete than before. Yusif could see a huge lake, visible in all directions as far as the eye could see, calm and indigo blue. From the centre of this lake, a barren island emerged, water cascading from it, disturbing the lake's seeming tranquillity. From the desolate earth, all kinds of vegetation began to grow wildly, until it became a land, both rich and fertile. The evolution of the island didn't stop there… as though watching a time-lapsed video, it continued to change with buildings and people materialising as time passed.

As Yusif looked down upon the island, he could now see three, large, crystalline pyramids, set centrally in a wide clearing, surrounded by fully cultivated fields and beyond them, a dense forest. Two pyramids were side by side, with a passageway running between them, leading to the third, larger pyramid, behind them. The surfaces of the pyramids looked smooth, except for the stairways carved into the structures, which led to open doorways. Each pyramid reflected the light of the sun, manifesting rainbow hues, that shimmered in the air around and above them. Nearby, Yusif could also see two smaller, tower-like structures, also glistening in the sunlight.

The fields directly behind the pyramids were filled with a myriad of produce; colourful vegetation created a patchwork of squares, separated only by the natural walkways and flattened pathways created by the peoples' feet, as they regularly tended their crops. In the centre of some fields, Yusif could see that natural springs had found their own meandering channels, branching off here and there, allowing the life-giving water to reach the vegetation, encouraging it to flourish.

As Yusif continued to experience the vision, he instinctively sensed that the vegetation was grown and used, not only to feed the populace, but to create medicines for healing and curing any ailments the people of the island contracted.

Yusif watched the people of the island, going about their daily lives. Like small dots moving up and down the pathways between the fields, milling around the bases of the crystal pyramids, as well as those entering and leaving the buildings via the stairs. He intuitively knew, that some of the people lived within the pyramid structures and that the buildings served three purposes, as living quarters, treatment areas and as schools. He had a clear feeling and understanding that all those on the island, lived as one big community. There was a beautiful feeling of peace and harmony coming from the land and its inhabitants.

As Yusif bathed in the feelings of well-being, peace and harmony, he was abruptly taken aback, as suddenly, an ominous darkness began to spread over the island. As the darkness cast its shadow over the land, the inhabitants fled the fields they were tending, to take shelter within the pyramids, from which, they never re-emerged. Nature began to take back the land. The fields and pathways became overgrown and it was hard to tell where one ended and another began and they all withered and died, as the life-sustaining natural springs dried up. The pyramids became encrusted with a rock-like material and began to look more like mountains and hills, rather than the beautiful buildings they once were. The land soon became a place of darkness and decay, covered by a thick and seemingly impenetrable dark cloud. Strangely, the darkness did not extend over the lake from which the island had been born, only the island was obscured.

Yusif was saddened and worried by the rapid turn of events he was witnessing. The despair he started to feel, however, was quickly replaced by fear, as he felt himself suddenly being pulled away from the vision; drawn upwards, further away from the island, which grew smaller as he rose. Now looking down at the island from a greater height, he realised there was a new perspective being shown to him and his initial fear turned to intrigue.

From his new position, Yusif could also see seven spiritual beings, who, like himself, were hovering over the island. All that Yusif could discern of the spiritual beings, was that they had a vaguely humanoid shape, with indistinguishable features, as though they were obscuring his ability to recognise or memorise their details. Even their clothing was ethereal, however, each of the beings did radiate light, each light being one of the colours of a rainbow and this detail aroused Yusif's curiosity. *Who were they? Where did they come from? Why were they here? Were they responsible for the all-consuming shadow? What was the significance of the colours they radiated?* All these questions and more, sped through Yusif's subconscious mind, questions to which he felt he must find the answers. As these thoughts were racing through his mind, he peered closer, realising that each spirit was, in fact, holding an object, from which the coloured light was shining brightly. As he made the connection between the light and the object, feeling like he might be close to getting answers, the beings began to release the objects, letting them drop away, one by one, toward the island and the shadow that veiled it. Red, orange, yellow, green, blue, indigo and finally violet, streaked through the ether, gathering momentum, as they fell into and beneath the dark cloud. As the lights penetrated the cloud, each of the beings faded away, leaving Yusif with more questions than answers. As the last being disappeared from view, Yusif watched as his vision of the beings and the island begin to fade. His mind's eye was closing and his consciousness returned to his physical body.

He kept his eyes closed, trying to see more; to keep a hold of the vision, willing it back into his mind's eye, wishing it hadn't ended. He wanted answers to questions that he knew he was going to be asking himself. Reluctantly, Yusif opened his eyes and sat there pondering about this vision, not sure what to make of it. He needed to capture the essence of it before any of the detail faded from his memory. So, he reached across to the small table next to him and picked up his meditation journal and pen, deciding that on one page he would write down, in as much detail as possible, what he remembered seeing in his vision and on the following pages, he would try to analyse what he thought the elements of the vision might mean. Once he had figured out their meaning, he would tick them off. So far, this vision didn't have any ticks next to it. He was not sure if the vision was passing on a symbolic message or whether it was insight or foresight into actual events. He put the book back on the table and decided to leave it for now. He could ponder some more about what it could possibly mean, as he waited for some kind of inspiration to enlighten him. Yusif did not know it at the time, but that day and that vision, was going to be the start of a life-changing adventure.

YUSIF

Yusif was a slender man, with a quiet manner and a softly-spoken voice. He'd reached the age of twenty-seven and was still waiting to meet his future wife, who would be with him on his life's journey. He had lived under the care of his grandfather, from the age of four, since both Yusif's parents had passed into the hereafter and however sad that was, it was his grandfather he had to thank for the understanding of life and living, that he now carried.

His grandfather had taught him wisdom, built on a foundation of love and understanding, using a mixture of philosophies from around the world, with the main source of this understanding coming from the verses and teachings of *The Quran*. All that he had learnt, had formed the foundation that shaped his well-balanced manner.

Part of Yusif's morning routine was to have a cup of coffee and spend a bit of time pottering about. He would do a little reading or writing, depending on how he was feeling, then he would make his way to his meditation room at the top of the house. This is the place where he would begin and end each day. There was not much furniture in this room. In one corner, there was a small table holding a lamp and his meditation journal. In another corner was another table where he had placed a few miscellaneous items he had picked-up on his travels. There was nothing of any real value, however, they gave him pleasant memories of places he had travelled. Next to the table was a bookshelf, containing Yusif's personal book collection.

Hanging on the wall above the bookshelf was a photograph from his childhood days and in the middle of the room was his prayer mat, close to a small heater.

Yusif would always have three meditative sessions per day – morning, afternoon and evening. He would make his way to the room at the top of the house, where he would turn his attention inward and prepare himself to attain mindful self-awareness. He would use that time to cultivate his inner awareness, using reflection, remembrance, examination, contemplation, deliberation and pondering to understand his purpose in life. It was from this place that his inner voyage of self-discovery had started, many years previously and which he liked to call, 'a journey into the rainbows.'

A week after experiencing the strange vision, at around 11 o'clock in the morning, Yusif was standing in front of his sitting-room window, staring at nothing in particular, as he reflected on the five years it had been since his grandfather had passed away. There were still times when he missed his grandfather's presence around the house. Some days were easier than others, as memories of him found their way to the front of his mind. However, he would not change a single second of the time that they had spent together.

A smile appeared on Yusif's face, as he remembered a time when he was around ten years old. He came home from school to see his grandfather sitting peacefully in his chair. In fact, he was sitting too peacefully. He tiptoed over, reached out and put his hand in front of his grandfather's nose to see if he was still breathing. To his dismay, he felt no air exhaling from his nose or mouth. For the first time in his life, Yusif felt a lump in his throat, as his emotions filled and overwhelmed him with fear and grief. With what little knowledge he had at that age, he decided to check for a pulse. He lifted his grandfather's hand, which was limp, as if there was no life in it. He tried to find his pulse but couldn't find one. *Maybe I am not holding his wrist in the right place*, he thought to himself.

His own heart was beating like a horse, racing at full gallop, while his breathing became rapid and his eyes began to fill with tears. He decided to try and feel for his grandfather's heartbeat. He slowly and apprehensively moved his hand towards his grandfather's chest, barely touching the cloth of his jubba, when his grandfather suddenly jumped in his chair and opened his eyes. So startled was Yusif, that he fell over backwards, ending up in a heap on the floor. His grandfather looked at him as Yusif sat there panting and gulping down air. Yusif wiped away his tears with one hand, then put it back down on the floor to keep his balance. His grandfather, as usual after a nap, wiped his face with his hands and then rubbed his eyes. He then wrapped his hands around the top part of his beard and pulled them down to the end. He repeated this move a couple more times, as he looked down at Yusif sat on the floor. This straightening of his beard was more of a habit than anything else but was his grandfather's way of always looking presentable, even when he was at home alone.

"Young kids nowadays, always rushing around. If you want some exercise, go and get me a drink of water," said his grandfather, as he continued to straighten himself in the chair and adjust his clothing. All Yusif could hear, as he looked up from the floor at his grandfather, were his own thoughts screaming in his head: *I thought you were....*

His grandfather could see that Yusif was flustered and quickly figured out what he was thinking. "Hello-o," his words, finally finding their way through the crowd in Yusif's head. "Hello, is anybody there? I would like a drink of water, if it is not too much trouble for you?" repeated his grandfather, with a smile on his face.

"I thought, I thought...," were the only words Yusif could utter, as he jumped up, ran to the kitchen and quickly came back with a glass of water. Yusif handed the water to his grandfather, while still reeling from the shock of his grandfather's abrupt awakening. Yusif smiled again at the memory and soon became lost within his own thoughts, beautiful memories and reminiscing about the time he'd had with his grandfather.

Sometimes, he would think about his parents and who they were, however, he could not remember their faces. He was only four years old when they passed over to the hereafter. The only memory he had of his early life and his parents, had almost faded from his mind. He remembered being around three years of age, full of energy and fearless, as he galloped around a table, riding his sturdy mount (a sweeping brush) laughing and shouting to his mother. He couldn't recall the words but the feeling of being loved and encouraged to use his imagination had stayed with him. His mother had caught a hold of him in mid-gallop and swept him up into her arms, placing him carefully on the wide windowsill and telling him to sit still and give a big smile, so that she could take a photograph of him, with his rosy cheeks, ruddier by his efforts as a jockey. Yusif has scrutinised the picture hoping to see the reflection of his mother in the photograph, which would have helped him to remember her in more detail, however, the angle at which the photograph had been taken, did not show her reflection. In his later life, he saw the picture as a going away present from his parents, as it was not too long afterwards, that they passed away. That same photograph was now hanging on the wall of his meditation room. Yusif was snapped out of his reverie by the harsh and unwelcome ringing of the telephone.

He walked over to the phone and picked it up.

"Hello," said Yusif.

"Hi Yusif," said the voice on the other end of the phone. He recognised her voice straight away, it was Alisha, his neighbour calling.

"We are on the motorway and the traffic is stopping, starting and moving really slowly. We will be home later than we planned. We are expecting...,"

The line went dead and Yusif didn't hear the last part of the message. He tried to re-dial the number but to no avail, so he placed the phone back on the receiver, thinking that Alisha would call back any time now. She didn't and, although perplexed by this event, Yusif realised it was time for his next meditation and put the worry to the back of his mind.

INTO THE RAINBOWS

Once Yusif reached the room at the top of the house, he prepared to start his meditation by organising the room, placing a jug of water and a cup on the table, turning on the lamp and preferring a dimly lit room for his daily meditations, drew the curtains to keep out the sunlight.

He sat down on his prayer mat and closed the 'windows to his soul' in prayer. He would always start with a prayer, as this would put him into a 'surrendered state of mind'. Once he had finished his prayer, he would start his meditation. This was a focused effort, to transcend thoughts about Earthly life, withdrawing his attention from his immediate surroundings. Lately, his inner journey had become much more concentrated and he felt a new kind of determination driving him onwards. In his previous meditations, sometimes he would feel himself travelling great distances. Other times, he would almost give up in despair as his mind filled with worldly thoughts. When he did push past the daily thoughts about worldly life, he could feel his consciousness expanding beyond the cage of his body and mindset, where he felt a beautiful calmness, which quickly removed all his unnecessary thought activity.

As he sat on his mat in meditation, from the corner of his inner vision, a light, like a shooting star, raced across what seemed to be the horizon. In the distance, other lights began to appear then disappear, their shapes reminding Yusif of snowflakes. Some of the intricately designed patterns would merge, forming a complete light that drifted off into the distance, while others grew in beauty, changing to different colours as they passed closely by him, a rainbow of snowflakes.

There appeared a small, bright light, in the centre of Yusif's vision. It had a piercing brightness, much more radiant than the other lights he could see. It was beautiful and beheld his vision and attention. During all this inner activity, he began to feel himself travelling forward, although physically, he had not moved. A childhood memory flashed across the screen of his mind and Yusif instantly knew that the piercing light he could see, was the entrance to a place he vividly remembered entering as a child. As he watched, he saw an image of himself as a small child falling to sleep. His small body rose up from a bed and floated towards the light. From a lying position, he awoke and was now standing upright. The small boy set off running directly towards the light, passing through to the other side.

The recollection made him feel more adventurous and wanting to find out more, so he ventured on. As he focused on this light, it appeared to grow in size, either it was coming closer to him or he was travelling towards it and, as it got closer, he could feel its warmth on one side of his face, while on the other side, there was a soft and gentle breeze. This light surrounded him and began to fill his vision.

Once he was filled with the piercing light at the centre of his vision, he felt a strange sensation. He could feel himself moving and gently swaying from side to side, he could also hear a sound, like a strange buzzing frequency. It was too high for Yusif to clearly understand its meaning. He instinctively knew they were voices trying to speak to him, but he was unable to make sense of what was being said. After a few anxious moments, Yusif felt himself rising from the floor and coming to a stop. He opened his eyes to find he was inches from the ceiling, he knew something strange had happened. He looked around the room from his new perspective, intrigued by the fact that he could see himself, still seated on his prayer mat below his present position and eventually realised that he was floating directly above his physical body. He put his hands on the ceiling and pushed himself back down towards the floor. Floating down and twisting himself, he landed on the floor next to his physical body. Standing there, he looked at himself. He had heard about others who'd had out of body experiences but their words did not nearly describe the real experience of it. Although he could not see his spirit body, he knew his appearance and shape was an exact replica of his physical body. Walking around his body as it sat on the mat, was a strange experience. He took in a deep breath, expecting to see the chest of his physical body expand. Nothing happened, nothing at all.

At that same moment, his mind raced back in time, to when he came home from school and saw his grandfather sitting, very still, in his chair. He vividly remembered that moment because it was the first time he had ever felt afraid and of not knowing what to do in a scary situation.

Well, grandpa, you did not tell me about this. Were you outside your body on that day I came home from school? he thought to himself.

He heard a voice start speaking to him, as he stood there looking at his body sitting on the prayer mat.

"Yes, he used to come to our world quite often. Are you curious about what has happened to you?" asked the voice.

"Yes," said Yusif, as he stood there, looking around his room, trying to find the source of the voice.

"You have transferred a greater part of your consciousness into one of your spiritual bodies. These bodies are replicas of your physical body and they are like ships, you use them as a means of transport, for sailing the great spiritual oceans," explained the voice that he could hear but not see the speaker.

Yusif stretched out his arms and saw his spirit form for the first time. His arms were made of light, weirdly transparent yet obvious in their outline. He looked down at his legs and they were also made of light. As he was looking at his spiritual body, realising he was naked, there materialised garments around his body. He reached down and could feel his spirit body and clothing with his hands, everything felt incongruously solid to the touch. His appearance and clothing matched his own self-image and as he stood there in his room, looking around to see who was speaking to him, he was surprised to see only himself sitting there. He looked at other things in the room and realised how dull everything in the physical world appeared.

"Life goes on after the death of the physical body," the voice continued, as it somehow knew what Yusif was thinking about. "There is a thread of energy, like an umbilical cord, which allows the spirit to stay connected to the physical body, similar to the way a mother and her child are connected during pregnancy. What you call death, occurs only once this connection is spiritually severed."

On hearing this, Yusif thought he had better get back into his body. He felt that he was not ready to cross over to the other side. He had many things he wanted to do in his life. He walked over to his meditating body and found he could enter the physical entity as he placed his feet within the sitting Yusif and started to lower himself down into it. He was almost back in his body when a spirit form appeared.

This form was also made of light. Yusif had met many people in his life and this soul was not someone that he recognised. It had kind eyes and a radiant face with a loving smile. Because there was no threat or anything to be afraid of, Yusif smiled and kept calm.

"Not so fast, my friend," said the being of light.

Yusif stopped and rose out of his physical body again. As he separated himself from his body, he could not help thinking how wet and heavy it felt, it was like being caught out in a heavy rainfall, you know, the ones that completely soak you, right through to the skin, where on arriving home, only when you have taken off the soaking-wet overcoat and clothing, changing into dry, loose, casual clothing, can you feel refreshed and free from the heaviness of the wet clothing.

"It is not yet your time. You have many more years left in the physical world. You will reach a good age before you return to us. Why not look around while you are free of your physical body?" suggested the voice.

"Good idea," replied Yusif, as he started to walk around the room.

As the room was sparsely furnished, used only for meditation and not much else, Yusif looked once more at himself sitting on the mat, he decided to go downstairs, as his curiosity was piqued. He walked over to the door and stood in front of it for a moment. He reached out to grab the handle so he could venture out, but his hand passed right through the door handle, so he just stared at it perplexed.

"What are you waiting for?" prompted the voice, which was now coming from behind him.

"How do I open the door?" asked Yusif. He was still in his Earthly mind when it came to doors.

"Hold out your hand," instructed the voice.

Yusif took a step back and held out his hand.

"Now, take a step forward and push against the door, not the handle, the wood of the door itself," continued the voice.

Holding his hand out, Yusif took a few steps forward and to his surprise, his hand passed through the wooden door. He turned his head around and smiled, as he remembered... he was now in the spiritual world!

He pulled his arm back and looked at it, turning it over and back again, nothing had changed, his arm was still intact. Gaining confidence, he stepped forward again, this time, pushing his head through to the other side of the door. *So far, so good*, he thought. Following through with the rest of his body, he felt a strange sensation, a low vibrating energy that seemed to be trapped within the wood. Yusif could feel it interacting with his body, a little tension perhaps, a bit like a light shower of fine rain, slightly pressing on his spiritual self, but eventually giving way and allowing him to pass through. He turned around to look at the door he had inexplicably been able to pass through and it was exactly as it was before he left the room, closed and inert. Shrugging his shoulders, he turned back and began to make his way down the stairs.

He had to be sure that he was not dreaming, so he looked around for anything unusual. He went into the main living room at the front of the house, trying to ignore his familiarity with the furniture and décor, still looking for anything incongruous, eyes scanning, floor to ceiling and wall to wall, even going as far as laying down on his stomach to peek underneath the furniture. Then he spotted it, underneath the chest of drawers, towards the back, near the skirting board and an unused plug socket, there was an old letter. It must have slipped down the back of the chest at some point in the past and he'd never known it was there. He made a mental note to check for the letter again, once he had finished his meditation and returned to his physical body.

Yusif thought it strange that his parents and grandfather weren't there, in this spiritual plane. His own thoughts and preconceptions told him that he should be in Heaven and that all those nearest and dearest to him should also be there, however, he was alone in his house, except for the spirit being that was speaking to him. A thought in the back of his mind came rushing forward. He wanted to see his grandfather and visit Heaven, wherever and in whatever direction they were in.

ON THE OTHER SIDE

Now that Yusif didn't have a physical body, he felt he had much more clarity of thought and awareness. He knew he could think beyond the limitations his physical body and mind imposed on him.

"If you want to join us, fill yourself with love," said the voice.

There was one thing that his grandfather had taught him; he knew that through the expression of love, a light would manifest and the 'Spiritual Law of Attraction' would carry him to wherever he wanted to go. There was only one place he wanted to go – Heaven.

"Believe in love," said the voice.

Yusif took one last look around his front room, clasped his hands together, closed his spiritual eyes and thought about what love meant for him.

Again, a bright light came into view. He watched, as the light got brighter and completely filled him. He felt himself travelling in a forward direction with great speed, subconsciously knowing that the being speaking to him was traveling right beside him, guiding him on the journey. After what felt like only a few moments, there was another sudden burst of light, he could perceive through his closed eyelids.

This is exhilarating, Yusif thought to himself.

His forward rush came to a gentle end, accompanied by a tingling sensation all over his body. He didn't know how far he had travelled but having felt the forward momentum come to a stop, he opened his eyes to find he was standing in a radiant, bright light. There was a tremendous and euphoric feeling of love flowing through the atmosphere, which made Yusif feel calm and content. It was so fulfilling and complete; the place he had left, seemed like a million miles away. The thoughts he had about his life in the world, had almost faded from his mind, even the fact that he had a physical body, was almost forgotten.

Yusif suddenly became aware that they were not alone. The being traveling with Yusif faded once they had come to a stop. Other beings had joined them. He sensed there were four beings, two male and two female. They were just outside the field of his vision, so any distinctive features were not plainly visible. What he could see of them was a silhouette and basic facial features, within a radiant shimmer.

"*As Salamu Alaikum* (peace be upon you) my friends," said Yusif.

"*Wa alaikum as-salam* (and upon you be peace)" was the reply, from the four mystical beings of light.

"Who are you?" asked Yusif.

"We are your companions while you are here," was their reply.

"What are your names?" Yusif asked.

The same reply came back to Yusif.

"We are your companions," the beings of light repeated.

A smile appeared on all their faces and Yusif now realised that the answer to any more questions like that, would only elicit the same response.

In the distance, Yusif could hear the muted sounds of music playing, the melodies and its expression were beautiful and soothing, as it filled the atmosphere. Yusif had heard music like this before but only for short moments. When he did not have too much to do, he would sit down and strum on his guitar. Being a bit of a musician himself, there were times when he was playing his guitar that inspiration came to him, opening his awareness; his mind would fill with additional melodies and lyrics that accompanied the music as he sang and played his guitar. This music that he heard, was not heard by his physical ears, it was much deeper than that.

"Where are we?" asked Yusif. One of the females of the group stepped forward.

"We are in one of the many Heavenly worlds that exist. We are your first point of contact while you are visiting this realm. We are its caretakers."

Yusif stood there looking around, but all he could see was light.

"Come my friend, let's walk," said another of the females of the group.

They started walking away and beckoned Yusif to follow them. He felt safe, so he moved among them. The ground beneath their feet began to slope downwards on a gentle decline, eventually passing through the mist that swirled around their feet, in the basin of a terrain. They began to climb up a hill, moving quickly not giving Yusif a chance to look around. Once they reached the top of the hill and were in the clear, the view before Yusif made him gasp. He was standing on a hilltop, looking down over a landscape of great beauty.

Yusif lived in the city of Bradford, a northern city in Yorkshire, most of his life. A city that has a diverse culture, which boasts a mixture of old and new architecture and infrastructure and has over twenty surrounding towns and villages, some of which are world heritage sites. Although Yusif knew he didn't have to travel far out of the city to be within the countryside, he rarely found the time to do so. He wasn't used to seeing so much space and greenery around him and this was one of the reasons he now found the vista before him to be so breath-taking.

I must make a mental note to get out to the countryside more often, Yusif thought to himself.

"What is the name of this place?" Yusif asked.

"Bakka," was the reply from the companion.

The beautiful blue sky sported a few patches of fluffy white clouds and other thinner clouds, like stretched cotton-wool balls, giving the heavens an ocean-like appearance. In the distance, on the horizon, there was a large lake, although it was difficult to tell the difference between the sky and the lake, unless you really looked, for you could not really tell where the skyline ended and the lake started. Yusif actually mistook the lake for an ocean at first, as it covered so much of the land. To the left, in the far off distance, was a mountain range, not of the magnitude of the snow-topped Himalayas, more akin to the peaks of the Pennines in the Yorkshire dales, as they were covered in greenery. Over to the right was a forest covering a part of the land which came to a stop and levelled out into a large grassland area. It looked like you could walk for miles and nothing much would change around you. To the left, there were cultivated fields laid out in a patchwork of large squares. He figured these were created by the inhabitants of the land. They looked similar to farmers' fields on Earth as he could see that they had been tilled and seeded. Every couple of fields had different kinds of crop, creating a multitude of colour, making the landscape beautiful to look at.

Travelling around on foot in Bakka, was swifter than in the physical world, allowing you to cover greater distances, with little effort. As though each step was a leap but without the associated height, amazing! They all made their way down the pathway that ran between the hillsides, stopping about halfway down to take in the magnificence of the variety, beauty and rainbow of colours displayed by the flowers and plants that filled the landscape and the hillside. Around the smaller rocks, up the hillside, were flowers of all kinds, giving each rock a majestic appearance; each type of flower was radiant, with some having petals of two, three or more colours. The fragrances that they released filled the atmosphere, adding to the freshness of the valley. Yusif took in a deep breath through his nose, filling his lungs, feeling like he had walked into a flower shop when the flowers were blossoming at their fullest. As he exhaled, the freshness of his breath was like the flowers all around him. He himself, became filled with the scent of the flowers.

Even the moss covering some of the rocks looked like a perfectly trimmed garden lawn. He saw unfamiliar plants and vegetation that were also a multitude of colours, some with great depth and other larger flora and fauna where he could see energy moving through the veins of the petals and leaves. This created a glow around each of them and around the outer edges of the flowers, the energy would arch and swirl as if it were prostrating. Standing there and taking in all the beauty, filled Yusif with awe. This place was nothing like the Earthen plane. It was so much more vibrant and colourful and added to the land's radiant beauty.

In the periphery of his vision, he could see the flowers swaying from side to side in the gentle breeze. He turned and watched as dainty, colourful birds fluttered from one flower to another. Beautiful plumage, shimmering in the sunlight, multi-toned feathers, flashing as the sun caught them at different angles. Yusif was mesmerised as they toiled to gather the nectar. As he watched more closely, he saw a phenomenon he had never before seen or noticed in nature. There was a quiet, yet noticeable melody in the air, as though the birds and the flowers were communicating in song and, to Yusif's surprise, he discovered he could understand their language. They seemed to treat each other with respect, only drinking up the sweet tasting nectar after asking God and the flower for permission to do so and after each partaking, the birds would give thanks and praise to God, with gratitude to the flowers themselves. They would flit from flower to flower, taking sips of nectar, pollenating as they went.

As Yusif looked closely at the ground, he noticed that the insects scurrying through the undergrowth were aware of their tasks. They each enjoyed the fruits of their deeds. He watched as they contentedly rummaged through the undergrowth and soil, making little noises, as if they were chattering to themselves. When they met one of their own, they would pause their foraging tasks to perform a short dance, where the smallest of motion had meaning, communicating through movement and gestures rather than vocal expression. Yusif felt a sudden burst of realisation – most species of animals form communities like that of humankind, each having their own way of living and communicating. The human spirit is but one of the thousands of creations of God. Each community performed tasks that supported and helped the others in their growth and development. In this, Yusif realised that the inspiration, mercy and forgiveness of God, really did reach the very depths of His creations. It also made

Yusif more aware that God is knowledgeable about the smallest to the largest of His creations.

Turning back to continue his exploration of this amazing environment, Yusif was just about to step onto the grass, when one of his companions touched him lightly on the shoulder and pointed in the direction of a tree that was nearby. To his amazement, a smiling face peered out from the tree trunk. Yusif made his way over to the tree and looked into the pleasant face of the spirit revealed in the bark. The spirit welcomed Yusif to the island and then disappeared back into the trunk.

"Excuse me?" asked Yusif politely.

The face of the spirit within the tree reappeared.

"Hello, give me a moment, please..." replied the tree spirit.

The branches of the tree began to shake a little, as the tree spirit stepped out of the tree. This made Yusif step back a little to get out of the way. It was an exact replica of the tree, including the height, leaves, branches and fruit, however, it shrank down to become a similar height to Yusif and his companions. Yusif noticed that when the tree spirit stepped out, there was a slight change in the colour and the glow around the tree itself.

"Who are you?" asked Yusif.

"Why I am a tree spirit," was the reply. "Everything you see has a spirit. Each tree is presided over by an individual being. Even the blades of grass are cared for by a spirit being. All life, including your own has a spiritual core or essence. All life contains a light, through which it receives guidance and sustenance from God. We are all here as caretakers of God's creation. You have a physical body back on Earth?"

"Yes," replied Yusif.

"Make sure you take care of it. Your body is the instrument you use to help you become aware of your own inner depth, physical and mental capabilities. Each of us must become aware of why we have a body. We all have to question what we use our body for. Do you use your body as a vehicle through which you strive to perfect yourself?" The tree spirit asked Yusif, as it gently swayed from side to side.

"Yes, still working on the perfecting bit," replied Yusif.

"To have made it here, you are of those who understand that the body and its mind can allow you to see, in a safe environment, your darkness and your light," explained the tree spirit.

"Some, in our world, recognise this truth, however, some are not aware of their real purpose. They turn away from their true centre. They do not always listen to the inspiration that comes to them from the Heavens," replied Yusif.

"How do you find this true centre?" asked the tree spirit.

"The most direct way is the practice of meditation. We apply our thinking, feelings and willpower to create and manifest certain thoughts within our mind. We express our feelings of love, which opens us up to receiving and creating beautiful, loving thoughts. We each learn to hold ourselves steady, within the feelings of love. Through our expression of love, our inner light shines. The light removes the darkness that surrounds us. Through the light we are able to pass through the door that allows us to reach higher states of Heaven. Many are striving to see beyond the influences of the worldly life. Slowly, we are beginning to awaken from our sleep. The light we see during our meditations, is God's way of guiding us out of the darkness and into the light," said Yusif, as he explained the very basics of meditation to the tree spirit.

"Your journey still continues in Bakka. It does not end once you come here. The life of the hereafter is a continuation of the Earthly life, of the world on which you live. Your Earthly life allows you to purify the darkness that flows into your mind. As you grow, you transcend in conscious awareness," said the tree spirit.

"Our world is a very dense world. Our physical bodies reduce our connection to the hereafter to a flicker. Many only believe in what they see and accomplish in the physical world. There are some souls that have completely cut themselves off."

"Yes, we are aware of the Earth and some of its difficulties," acknowledged the tree spirit.

"Many great teachers have been sent to the Earthly plane. It is from their teachings, that religious institutions have formed. Each organisation supporting its own followers, as they strive to know the truth concerning their life on Earth," explained Yusif.

"We all watch with hope, as you each come up struggling for your own self. Well, it has been a pleasure speaking with and listening to you, thank you. May you enjoy your time in Bakka," said the tree spirit, with a smile and a long blink of its eyes, to show its pleasure in the conversation.

The spirit being stepped back into the tree, which then returned to its original glowing radiance. Its face was the last thing to disappear back into the trunk.

Getting down on his knees, Yusif looked at the grass, focussing on a single blade. To his surprise, just like with the tree, a small face appeared. He could see a small aura of light radiating around the blade of grass. He lowered himself into a crouching position and looked at a wider patch of grass. He had to rub his eyes and look again at the appearance of many, tiny, smiling faces. He could see that their light energy was inter-connected, which gave him an understanding that there is no separation, only oneness and unity. From spirit beings to animals, plants and minerals, each kingdom's energy interacted with the other. Yusif stood up and looked across the valley. As his understanding expanded, so did his vision penetrate yet another veil. The whole place became filled with spiritual beings, tending and protecting God's creations. Like the tree spirit, each being was an exact replica of the creation they were looking after.

He watched, as the opening of the veil and spirit of inspiration swept across the valley. Like the ripples on the surface of a pond when struck by a falling pebble or rock, all the spirits within the land felt the presence of this energy. This wave of energy cleansed, purified and supplied sustenance to every being and every form. Even the rocks, leaves and petals praised God for their existence and sustenance; their loyalty and obedience putting the humblest on Earth, to shame. As the energy traversed the vista, the flowers released their exotic fragrance. He could feel the valley sigh and quench its thirst. With bated breath he could feel the whole valley breathe, as it reached out to receive its sustenance. In Bakka, everything was aware of its connection to God. It was nothing like the density of his world and the enmity that exists between each of us. In that moment, Yusif knew that he was experiencing something very special. The veil to this inner dimension closed and his vision returned to only seeing the outer form of the land he was visiting. They continued to walk along the pathway until they reached the bottom of the hill.

"We have a number of things to take care of, so we will leave you to explore on your own for a while," said his companions.

"Will you be back?" enquired Yusif.

"Yes, we will not be long. If you need us, just think to yourself, where are my companions? We will be with you in a matter of moments," they said.

"Okay, I think things will be fine if I stay on this pathway," said Yusif, as his companions faded away.

Yusif then turned and continued walking, looking around and admiring the beauty of the land, feeling the warmth of the sun on his face, tempered by the gentle breeze of energy that kept the atmosphere fresh and making the temperature of the land he was visiting perfectly balanced.

ON THE BEACH

Yusif reached the top of a hillside that overlooked more of the land and as he started to walk downhill again, he could see that the single pathway split into two. One veered off to the right and one to the left. From where he was, Yusif could see that following the right-hand path would take him in the direction of the multi-coloured glow that could be seen over the lake. The left-hand pathway headed in the direction of some buildings and strange looking structures that were rising to the skyline. He was not sure what they actually were as he was too far from them to really see more details.

He started to follow the left-hand pathway to try and discern what the buildings and other structures were and as he got a little closer, they began to look like some kind of light beam radiating upwards from the ground into an ever-widening shaft of light, similar to the effect seen when using a torch, narrow at the base and wide at the top. As he got closer, he could see that there were twenty or thirty of these rays of light, some of which radiated colour. Yusif could not imagine what these could be. In the vicinity of the lights, he could see what appeared to be the rooftops of buildings, spaced out sporadically and he figured these might be the rooftops of farmhouses in the area.

Yusif considered continuing on this path, heading towards the columns of light but changed his mind. He was new to this land, he did not want to meet anyone without his companions by his side, so he decided to turn back and follow the right-hand pathway which led to the glowing, rainbow lake instead. As he made his way in the new direction, he noticed that the rocks scattered across the pathway had begun to change from granite, sandstone and shale to be interspersed with crystalline rocks and into fully formed crystals. He picked one up from the ground and confirmed his opinion that it was a crystal, as he had a number of his own at home that he had collected on his travels.

As he headed towards the lakeside and beachy shore, he thought the rainbow colours looked like they were sat on top of the water, radiant and glowing, slightly swaying from side to side, as if affected by the wax and wane of the lake tide, noticing that they reached right up to the skyline, like the lights he saw earlier.

It was not too long before the pathway he followed, led to a beach of soft, light-brown sand. Yusif was the only person at the beach, so he decided to take off his shoes, holding them in his hand and stepping onto the sand, where he felt the soft, warm grains envelop his feet, creating a feeling of warmth and comfort. He looked around the beach and saw yet more crystals, of differing sizes and shapes; some were solitary, but others were in small stacks and piles. He walked across the beach to explore further, feeling the slight resistance, as his weight pushed down into the sand, compacting and moulding to the shape of his feet. He found this a strange sensation to experience, as his movement prior to reaching the beach, felt more like he was drifting along rather than having a physical impact. He concluded that his spirit body 'wanted' him to feel the soothing and relaxing nature of the environment. Yusif bent down to grab a handful of sand, its texture feeling like the finest, quality silk and not coarse like Earthly beaches. He let the sand trickle through his fingers, noting that as the sun caught the grains of sand in motion, they flickered, like little stars falling from the Heavens, as they landed back on the ground.

Yusif meandered over to some crystals that were stacked up on the beach. As he got closer to them, he wondered who had stacked them. After walking around them, he decided to sit down on the sand. He placed his shoes by his side and looked out over the water as he marvelled in awe at the rainbow colours which were radiating from the middle of the lake. Closing his eyes and taking a deep breath, he listened to the soothing, rhythmic pattern of the small waves breaking on the beach. As he was enjoying his moment of tranquillity and calm, a voice spoke to him.

"Hello," said the voice.

Because of the gentile and beautiful way the voice said hello, Yusif was not startled by the sudden sound. He slowly opened his eyes and looked over to the stack of crystals, where he knew the voice had come from, to see a face next to the stack.

"I am a Crilarian," said the Crilarian.

"Hello," said Yusif, smiling and turning his body towards the stack of crystals, to face the spirit form.

The form moved to hover beside the stack. It took on a vaguely humanoid appearance while explaining that this form was the most appropriate way of engaging with those that came to Bakka. Further explaining, that in their plane of existence or world, they had a different form from what was being presented to Yusif. He noticed that the energy coming from the spirit was a mixture of both masculine and feminine energies, with a small electric arc-like streak of light, connecting the entity to the crystal stack. As the light arc moved to a different crystal segment, a new face appeared with its own voice and spoke through the energy form. Around the Crilarian faces, a small aura glowed like the rainbow on the lake. He watched as the energy moved around the top of its head, as if it too was prostrating from side to side.

"We are pleased you managed to complete the journey that brought you to the island," said the spirit form.

"Thank you, it's a pleasure to be here," replied Yusif.

"Tell us more about the world you come from," they requested with interest.

Yusif thought for a moment and replied, "It's beautiful. In our world, there are hundreds of different languages, cultures, customs and traditions. God, one of the names given to the universal spirit, allows us freewill to choose what we accept as the truth. Souls do exist together, although they are spiritually dwelling in different degrees of conscious awareness and in terms of growth and development, we are young and divided. Through our acceptance of wisdom, each soul must come up struggling for itself. During our short lives on Earth, we must learn to live together, expanding and developing ourselves. Through our learning and experiences, we make choices that allow us to grow in conscious awareness. The pathway leading to Bakka is found through loving surrender. It is a matter of finding a balance between the physical way of life and a spiritual way of life," explained Yusif, to the Crilarian.

"Each stack of crystals you see in Bakka, represents a group of spiritual beings, known as a soul group. We independently visit different worlds and bring our experiences back to the group to aid its understanding, growth and development. On some occasions we all visit one world at the same time, each of us going to a different land and culture within that world," said the Crilarian.

"Have you ever visited our world?" asked Yusif.

"No not yet. We have met a number of souls from your world and what they have told us about the Earth plane, makes it sound like an ideal opportunity for our development. The things we would learn and bring back to the group would aid our ascension. We await our time and when the opportunity comes, we will select one or more from our group to visit," said the Crilarian.

"Our world is one of the lowest vibrating planets in our solar system. It takes a lot of work to expand in awareness. There have been many great spiritual teachers that have come to the world to teach us the way. We are slowly beginning to awaken from the surrounding illusion that limits our conscious potential," explained Yusif.

"That is precisely why we think visiting your world would be of great benefit to our group," said the Crilarian, as it stood there radiating and sparkling with light.

"Do you see that crystal over there? The one that is unblemished and pure?" asked the Crilarian, gesturing in the direction of the crystal.

Looking across the beach in the direction suggested, Yusif could see what appeared to be a light sparkling in the distance.

"Yes," replied Yusif.

"That crystal arrived in our world thousands of your earth years ago. It came from one of the worlds in a higher vibration. You will not find another crystal like it in this land," said the Crilarian.

"Who brought it here?" Yusif queried.

"It was brought here, by a stranger from your world. He was one of your master teachers. He did not stay here for long, he came, left the crystal and then he was gone. We are waiting for the arrival of two more special crystals. We know where the crystals will appear. What we do not know is what needs to be done to create the conditions to make them appear," said the Crilarian.

"What kind of quest would one possibly need to complete in this land? It's so perfect here," said Yusif.

"All we know, is that there is a place in Bakka that needs to be restored and once this quest has been completed, two new crystals will appear. The energy the three crystals release when they are combined, will raise the vibrations of Bakka, making the Heavens above become available to those who strive," said the Crilarian.

A new form appeared and continued the conversation where the previous speaker left off.

"The energy of this new vibration will manifest a new colour, which will appear in the rainbow here and, eventually, in the rainbows of your physical world. The new energy will be filled with wisdom. From this new Heavenly abode, seeds of wisdom will inspire those who reach out with their consciousness, creating a curiosity that will make people seek to gain access to this new world. The wisdom will allow them to learn and retrieve greater insights into the words of wisdom, contained within the spiritual teachings of the holy books like *The Quran, The Bible* and *The Taurat*. Through the sharing of this wisdom, many will start to question what they have been taught to believe as the truth. They will strive to reach out and know for themselves. They will seek access to this higher wisdom and refuse to live in the darkness that has enshrouded their consciousness awareness. This wisdom will provide them with answers to their silent prayers and questions. As they meditate, they will feel this energy flowing through them. This new land that will be restored will eventually become their permanent home," said the Crilarian.

"That is interesting," said Yusif.

How many Crilarians are connected to this group of crystals? Yusif wondered to himself, as another face appeared.

"That depends on the group," said the next Crilarian that had just appeared.

"Hey!" exclaimed Yusif, as he laughed out and smiled. "You read my thoughts!" he said.

"Nothing is hidden in Bakka," said the Crilarian.

"Hearing something, knowing something and experiencing what you know, really does make you question the physical limitations of our world," said Yusif. "Once restored, what will the island be used for?" asked Yusif.

"That's a good question," said the Crilarian. "The island will be used by many different beings. They will live, work, develop and grow in awareness. In your world, the human soul is at the top of the conscious awareness tree. This makes many humans believe they are the only reason why the world was created. However, there are many other reasons for the existence of the Earth. Humanity is but one of many creations. There is an even greater reason why the world was created but at the moment, it is beyond the understanding of the human condition. Knowing such things would be of no use at this point in their evolution. There is much knowledge that God has kept back from humanity. Many fail to acknowledge even the smallest of spiritual matters. In time, inspiration will reveal a little more to those who seek it. With the restoration of the island, other beings from around this galaxy will also receive insights of inspiration from the newly created energy vibration," explained the Crilarian.

"Is inspiration sent to others in the same way we receive it on Earth?" asked Yusif.

"Yes, there is the spirit of inspiration. Every soul receives inspiration. There is one truth and the same spirit of inspiration speaks to all in the same way. Those who are ready, receive small flickers of information, which causes them to question their existence.

However, when this way is cut off because the fabricated worldly life has overshadowed the truth, some are shown signs and symbols through the physical form; they might notice certain things repeating in their life, to grab their attention. Part of that understanding is surrounded in what they know as synchronicity. Only those who are ready to see, will see," explained the Crilarian.

Yusif pondered for a moment, reflecting on the importance of listening to the inner inspiration. Yusif then received some thoughts within, from the spirit of inspiration that clarified a very important point. *Not listening is the same as turning your back on God's divine guidance.*

The Crilarian who was speaking, could see that Yusif had drifted off into his own thoughts, so waited for him to return to the conversation. Once Yusif had returned his gaze back in their direction, the Crilarian continued.

"Those that are ready will connect consciously to the essence of this new colour. The energy will purify them, cleansing and realigning them. In their meditative striving and openness to learning and change, they will gain insights into the wisdom stored within its vibration. As this loving energy establishes itself within the hearts and minds of those who strive, there will be an increase in the vibration of this colour. As the wisdom within the loving vibration is released, those who listen, as it imprints itself into their minds, will consciously ascend. They will be drawn up in stages, in nearness to those who reside within the Heavens. They will, in turn, pass on the inspiration they receive to others, so they may strive to reach this place. Knowledge of this new land will spread among a new generation on Earth. They will speak of the love that exists within this realm. Those who feel and see this colour will use it to deep clean, heal and transform that which has fallen out of balance. This knowledge will filter down and spread among those that doubt. At first, those who are blind will reject such knowledge. There will be a struggle between the darkness and the light. However, God has a plan. The light will win over the darkness. As some of this wisdom establishes itself in the minds of those who reside consciously in the lowest of the Heavens, they will start to slowly awaken. There will always be those who deny the truth. There will even be those who twist and turn it into something to fear. They can deny it all they want, however, the truth will slowly establish itself and they will eventually surrender to it," said the Crilarian.

"This new land sounds like it will be an amazing place," said Yusif, as he began to wish that he could visit it right away. At this point, he could only imagine what it would look like based on his short time in Bakka.

"Yes, this land and all that is within it, will be more exotic than the land you are at present visiting," said the Crilarian.

"How long will all this take?" Yusif asked.

"Only a select few are privileged to this information. We receive only that which we are capable of understanding. We know that those who complete their cycle on Earth, will eventually move to this new station. For some, it will take much soul searching. Those destined to move on to this new station will first live on the island that is waiting to be restored. From there, the ascension of souls to the new dimension will begin," answered the Crilarian.

Pausing for a moment, as the spirit of inspiration adjusted its flow, another voice continued.

"There are other worlds that exist in the lower vibrations and there are worlds above Bakka in higher vibrations of energy. Those who listened to their higher self while on Earth, are invited to move to higher Heavenly states. Their position in the hereafter depends on their willingness to surrender to the inner voice of wisdom. When they arrive in the hereafter, they continue their journey of development and service. The work that they are tasked with doing in the hereafter, will depend on their loving expression.

"Souls are tasked with many jobs once they arrive in the hereafter. The main area of work in Bakka is done in the crystal cave. As you go past the crystal cave and the farmlands, there is the city of Bakka. It is situated in a valley over yonder. Beings from all over come to live in the city of Bakka. Then there is the crystal structure on the lake. Those who live in the crystal structure, live and work everywhere.

Their tasks are greater than the majority of those who live and work in the city of Bakka."

Yusif looked across the lake in the direction of the rainbow. He could not see anything other than the rainbow on the lake.

"The crystal structure is always surrounded by a rainbow. Maybe you will get a chance to visit before you leave this land," said the Crilarian.

"Yes, it would be a great honour," said Yusif.

Yusif understood that there is both darkness and light that exists in life. He decided to ask another question, hoping they would shed some additional understanding to the knowledge he had.

"What of the ones on Earth who are not aware and refuse to believe in God?" asked Yusif.

"Another good question," said the Crilarian. "How we come to understand matters is as follows: some souls need certain lessons on Earth, to help them develop and grow. As a part of their development, their awareness is restricted to the daily routines of family life. The trials and tests within the family structure bring to the surface all that exists within them. This includes both their darkness and their light. Part of their experience on Earth is to learn to cope with the trials of loneliness and companionship, loss and gain, life and death. Those that strive to deal fairly during their experiences, working to mentally overcome their own darkness will achieve success. Their challenge is to use love, trust and truth to help them ascend into conscious awareness. Those who travel their journey alone, can but wait until God brings them together with a partner. We are aware life in the world is all about the material foundation, however, there are other realities. It is all about what is going on within themselves, rather than the external reality. The internal manifests itself into the external. Those who listen to their inner voice of guidance before acting, maintain a Heavenly hold on life. Their task is to be truthful in their dealings in the world. They will then receive a grand reward when they return home to the hereafter."

There was a moment of pause in the conversation, as Yusif reflected on the things he was hearing.

"Each soul continues their journey in the direction they lean toward in the mind. Those who refuse to surrender to the inspiration that is sent to them, will wish they had listened and paid attention. God forgives much of what each of us does, however, those who deliberately do not listen, after warnings have been given to them, will be marched in lines and transported to a place where the sun does not shine. God's ways do not change. God does nothing to harm anyone, they do it to their own souls. They harvest the seeds that fight against the truth they know. As their seeds of arrogance, ingratitude and selfishness grow, their hearts become hardened like a rock.

"Each soul has to look within themselves for the answers. Those who see their life as a struggle, will continue to do so, until they learn to surrender. They must see through the conditioning and strive to see their struggles as something to overcome. We must each work to transform our darkness into light. A measurement can and will be taken into account. That measurement is taken against the degree of the soul's attachment to its external surroundings. When a soul visits your world, they are given freewill and choice. Those who choose wisely, do not give themselves completely to anyone or anything. All those who return to this particular station in Heaven, fought hard in their meditations and rose above the irregularities that tried to hold them back. They listened to and chose to follow the best of their thoughts of inspiration," explained the Crilarian.

Yusif rested his elbows on his knees and brought his hands to rest under his chin. At the same time, he took a deep breath and exhaled. Yusif looked down at the golden-brown sand as curiosity about visiting the crystal cave and Bakka city was playing on his mind. He looked up to see his companions walking towards him.

"Thank you so much for your wise words. Your information has been very insightful. You have truly given me some insights that have increased my understanding." said Yusif to the Crilarian.

"Thank you again, for sharing information about life on your world," said the Crilarian.

Yusif could not help but wonder what they meant by the word 'again' in their sentence. He knew every word had its place but for some reason this word stood out in his mind. As far as he was concerned, this was the first time he had ever been to Bakka. Why would they say 'again' if it was his first time? Before he had time to query this matter, the Crilarians had faded away and were gone.

Yusif stood up and greeted his companions. His companions knew his inner thoughts but asked anyway.

"Would you like to visit the crystal cave?" asked one of his companions.

"Oh yes," said Yusif, with a smile on his face.

He rubbed his hands together and brushed the sand from his feet. He did not want any sand in his shoes. After dusting himself down to get rid of any sand that had stuck to his clothing, he joined his companions. They then made their way in the direction of the crystal cave. This is the place where crystals are grown, prepared then stored.

THE CRYSTAL CAVE

They arrived at the opening of the cave and Yusif could see that the inside of the cave was made of crystal with a floor so smooth, it looked almost like a clear pond without any ripples. In the centre of the cave floor was a large circular hole. Yusif could see other spirits stepping out over the edge of the hole and floating down. Walking to the edge, Yusif peered inside and he could see many spirits walking around. His companions stepped over the edge and began to float down to the ground. They looked up at Yusif as he watched them floating down. He was not too sure about stepping over.

Yusif sat down and shuffled himself to the edge of the circle with his legs dangling over the side. It reminded him of the first time he was taken to the swimming pool as a child. He sat there with his feet in the water, where all he did for about five minutes was to flick the water with his feet, as he watched everyone playing around and enjoying themselves. He had to work up his courage to lower himself further into the water. Once in, he was fine and soon started splashing around with all the other kids.

Yusif had no choice but to follow. He felt a little hesitant as he pushed himself off the ledge of the crystal floor, but then was amazed at how graceful the descent was. As he floated down, he was able to look over the whole area. The cave itself seemed to go on for as far as his eyes could see. Yusif was awed by the size of the crystal cave. It was the biggest indoor space he had ever seen and reminded him of a busy factory on Earth with hundreds of operatives going about their individual tasks; the cave was filled with thousands of spiritual beings busy working.

As Yusif's feet touched down, he looked back up at the hole in the ceiling, smiling at his initial reticence and secretly wanted to float down again. He joined the companions, who ushered him to follow them, where he was then introduced to Mario, who was the overseer, or as they like to be known, Crystaliers. Mario was a sparkling figure with many different colours swirling within his spirit body. Mario guided the visitors to his office, which was situated at a slightly higher elevation, on a platform that jutted out from the wall of the crystal chamber, affording Yusif the opportunity to view the chamber from a higher viewpoint.

Yusif was introduced to Mario's soul partner, Bev and he noticed that they were almost alike in their sparkling radiance but there were subtle differences you would miss if you did not look closely. It would be easy to get them mixed up at a first glance. They explained that it was their job to make sure the crystals were combined correctly ensuring the correct alignment of the energy within the crystals. Each of the crystals had to be perfectly aligned or it could not be used. Mario enjoyed welcoming visiting souls to the crystal cave, taking them on a short tour of the operation and pointing out specific areas of the chamber where certain tasks were completed, as the chamber was too big to see everything that was going on there.

"The majority of souls you see working here, are from the city of Bakka," explained Mario, "we also have additional souls from the higher dimensions. They come here to help with the alignment of some of the crystals they need in their worlds." As the tour progressed, Mario described the design of the crystal cave, arranged into seven levels, all similar in size and purpose. Each of the levels was divided into seven main areas and the only way you could tell there was a divide between the sections, was the large archways that partly protruded out from the wall and the ceiling of the crystal cavern. "On this level, there is an additional area known as the water chamber.

It is specifically for the preparation of crystals for a planet called Zamzam," said Mario, as they stopped outside a chamber filled with water, in the processing area. An eighth level was where the crystals were grown.

Mario then turned around and started to point out the different areas, explaining their purpose within the crystal cavern.

"The first section of the cave is the office and processing area. Through the first archway is the area where crystals are checked for quality and clarity, only keeping those with the right qualities to absorb energies. Next is the preparation area, where crystals are sorted by size and potential. Then there is the area where the crystals are cleaned. The subsequent sorting area is next in line, where the crystals go for frequency alignment and testing. They are then moved on to the inspection area, before the crystals are sent to the delivery area, waiting to be given to those who need them. Finally, there is the storage area, which is the largest area. All the beings that work in the cave keep their own crystals at their home. If they have to go away to perform tasks or further learning, they bring their crystals here for reprogramming and storing. They come to collect their crystals back when they return from their journeys. We also store other crystals for some of the spirits we know are visiting this realm. Some of the crystals are sent to the higher realms, some to the lower realms. Then there are those for the planet Zamzam."

"I've never heard of this planet called Zamzam," said Yusif, "what is so different about them and their crystals?" he enquired.

"Oh, the Zamureons look similar to humans in that they have the same body structure, with the majority of them having long, slender bodies, legs, arms and neck. They have a round head like a human head and here is where the main differences to human physiology can be seen. The top of their head extends to a bit of a point. The mouth area does not have any lips, making their face appear flatter than a human's face. It opens more from the top more than the bottom. Their eyes are laid back and slightly to the side of their head. This allows them to see almost three hundred and sixty degrees around themselves. When they blink, their transparent eyelids move from the bottom of the eye to the top, barely discernible, unlike human eyelids that are solid, blinking down then up as they fall and rise again. They have small holes as nostrils, just above their mouths. Their ears, like humans are at the sides of the head, but do not have any protruding parts like human ears, they are built into the bone structure of their skull. They look just like holes at each side of their head, however, they can change the direction of their hearing, by moving the holes forwards or backwards, depending on the direction they want to listen. When they speak to each other, in their natural language, they use a small amount of words, most of what they say is through clicking sounds that are made with their tongue and the back of their throat. Some of the more evolved Zamureons have learnt to speak in a way that makes it possible for us to understand them. The Hadzabe tribe in Africa speak using clicks to give you an idea of how they speak, however, the Zamureons use many more clicking sounds. These beings can live and breathe in water, like we breathe air. Their bodies are a variation of blue hues. They were created to be streamlined, enabling them to glide through the water without hindrance." Explained Mario.

"I would love to meet a Zamureon," said Yusif, "and what about their crystals? Do they differ at all?" he enquired.

"The crystals for Zamzam are created in the basement of the crystal structure on the lake. They are then moved to the lake where they are energised. Once energised, they are put into boxes and taken to the cavern in the crystal cave, where they are teleported to Zamzam. These crystals are of a different texture and quality from the others and are overseen and looked after in the lake, by Zamureons. The centres of some of the crystals are liquefied water and they are much lighter in mass than the heavier, mineral-based crystals of this land. Their outer texture is malleable, like a very bendy bubble. They are flexible and transparent, allowing one to almost see right through it. In our world they are very delicate. They are taken to Zamzam to be used as batteries are used on the Earthly realm, as they hold enough power to drive everything they need. Zamzam is also in the process of transforming; it's in the final stages of transcending and ascending to another dimension. All those that were ready, would be taken from the planet. The rest would have to stay behind."

"Wow!" exclaimed Yusif, "how very fascinating."

Mario continued to explain the functions of the other areas within the crystal cave, giving Yusif detailed insight into the intricacies of the crystals and how important they were to the many and varied planes of existence.

The checking area was for the newly arrived crystals. The majority of the crystals in the cave came from the eighth level, however, some were brought in from other dimensions and this was where they were laid out on long tables and visually checked for quality and clarity.

The sorting area was where certain crystals were grouped together and prepared for programming. Some of them would be used as healing crystals and were sorted to be placed with other crystals for healing. Teleporter crystals were put together with teleporter crystals, music, meditation, colour, protection and so on, were each grouped and put together on different tables.

In the preparation area, the crystals were prepared for frequency alignment. Some were fused together using energy, blended to treat deeply rooted spiritual conditions. Mario described the preparation process like baking a cake. First, you have to know and prepare your ingredients before you bake the cake. Certain crystal combinations were fused together to create special energies and frequencies for various beings and their spiritual needs. The vibrations of one crystal were raised, allowing it to pass through a more solidly-formed crystal. Once they were in position, the vibrations of the raised crystal were lowered again and this would cause both crystals to become fused with one another.

The preparation area was also a frequency amplification area. This was where the internal structural alignment of the crystal could be changed to hold higher frequencies. These altered frequencies would allow the crystal to amplify high-end or low-end energies. They could even be aligned to hold a mixture of energy vibrations. Much of the work done in this section was carried out by musically minded souls that understood sound vibrations and their healing uses. They were rechecked to ensure they were perfectly aligned and combined in the inspection area.

"There are beings from other worlds that work in this section. The human soul is not the only spiritual form," explained Mario, as they walked through part of the cavern.

Yusif watched as some of the spirit beings from the other worlds took on the colour of the crystals they were working with, changing as they moved around, tending different colours of crystal and reminding Yusif of chameleons; how they changed their colour to blend in with their environment.

In the inspection area, crystals were spread out on long tables, ready for Mario and Bev's team to inspect them. Their method of inspection was not visual, they would open their awareness as they walked down a line of tables, sometimes passing their hands over the crystals. Their inspirational awareness allowed them to pinpoint with great accuracy, the smallest of fractures or faults, removing those crystals to the defects conveyor belt. Specialist inspectors would then scrutinise the faults or fractures to see if they could be restored; nothing was wasted in this land and if it could not be restored, the defective crystals would be ground down into minute, sand-like particles, to be returned to the beaches of the lake. Some of the particles were taken by boat, to the crystal structure on the lake.

The storage area was the largest of all and contained the majority of the crystals. It was also the busiest area. There were thousands of tables in rows stretching the full length of the cavern. The most amazing thing to see was how each crystal was balanced on its own cushion of energy.

In the ceiling above those who worked in the storage area, were large circular tubes that looked like tunnels going up toward the sky, extending as far as the eye could see. In the hollowed out circular funnel tunnels, thousands of crystals were placed in their own little enclaves around the outer edges.

The circular holes in the floor went down through all the levels to the ground. Streams of energy from the ground level, flowed up and down through all the levels and continued up through the funnel tunnels. This also allowed souls to move between the different levels giving them access to the different floors. Using their minds, they could move up or down, forward or backwards, as they made their way.

These funnel tunnels also served as a gateway for those entering Bakka. Souls visiting from planet Earth and beyond, descended through these funnel tunnels. Each of the tunnels was continuously busy as souls fell asleep on Earth, they would arrive in Bakka, go straight to their crystal and as they looked into it, their daily activities were downloaded and stored. Yusif wondered to himself if these were the funnels he saw from a distance when he first came to the island. Mario confirmed to Yusif that they were visible from the outside.

Even though there were so many souls in this one place, it was a quiet place, as most of the communication took place telepathically. In certain areas and large gatherings, the newly arrived souls would speak verbally with their mouth and voice, however, they quickly adapted to telepathy once they arrived. It was still permitted to speak using verbal communication and some souls still enjoyed the verbal way of communicating.

Once the visitors from Earth had downloaded their information into their crystals, they would then go off to the libraries in different locations on Bakka, to educate themselves. When they returned to their bodies, any information, knowledge or spiritual messages would be received via their dreams as they slept.

Once Mario had given Yusif an overview of the crystal cave, they made their way back to the office area. Yusif thanked Mario for the tour. Yusif and his companions then left the cave and continued their journey to the city of Bakka.

CITY OF BAKKA

As Yusif and his companions approached the city of Bakka, he noticed a change in his awareness. The energy pulsations coming from the city felt lower in intensity and slower in cadence, to the surrounding area and especially that of the lake beach and crystal cave. Everything began to look a little duller in colour and as he looked back in the direction of the lake, he noticed that the rainbow was slowly disappearing. He also noticed that the crystals on the ground had changed to appear as normal stone rocks. Reaching the fields surrounding Bakka, the rainbow on the lake had completely disappeared. All he could see was the large body of water.

In the fields around Bakka, some souls were working the land as they did on Earth. The farms had all the usual animals you would expect to see, including cats and dogs. There were children playing in one of the fields, their laughter sailing through the air. Yusif watched, smiling, as they jumped and chased each other around in the field. It was explained to Yusif that pets remember those they stayed with on Earth and those that were loved, returned to be with their owners in the hereafter.

Once they had passed the outer fields surrounding Bakka, the hillside began to slope down into a valley. In the distance, Yusif could see the city of Bakka. It was situated within the beautiful valley and the buildings appeared to be well designed and spacious. The city was large and made some of the cities on Earth look small in comparison.

It was not long before they arrived in Bakka. It reminded Yusif of his life on Earth. The buildings and streets were exactly like those on Earth and there was even transportation for those who chose not to walk. For a moment he forgot he was in the hereafter as they walked down the streets. People in the city were dressed in everyday clothes. Most of the people appeared to be young. The souls that looked older, only appeared so because they had chosen to project themselves as being more aged. Yusif's companions explained that this city was one of many places where souls come to live. "Even in the Heavens below this station, there are lands and cities where souls live. These places have been created as a way of easing a soul's adjustment when it arrives in the hereafter." Yusif's companions also explained that when souls arrive in Bakka, they continue to work as part of their development. "That which exists in the lower Heavens, is by no means as beautiful as this station. This land and its landscape are by far, more radiant and beautiful to look at. So too, are its people more courteous of character.

"In the lower realm, the quality of life is darker. The buildings and the inhabitants express themselves in a more self-centred way. There is also a lack of knowledge and a reluctance to be of service. Those that live in the lower realms are not as courteous and friendly. Their main concern is about their own self. In the hereafter, souls are grouped together based on their spiritual expression and the 'Spiritual Law of Attraction'. Souls in this and every world have to work on themselves, in a bid to ascend and live in the Heavens above. The only way to ascend to a higher station is through the surrendering of one's own will self-desire. This restrains and purifies the soul of irregularities and enables them to ascend.

"Those who work in the city of Bakka do jobs of service, such as looking after new arrivals, helping them adjust to their new conditions. It is this unity of spirit and the doing of good deeds and not unity of religion or culture that brings souls together in the hereafter. Souls of like nature are brought together. There is no rivalry in the higher Heavens, souls become the best version of themselves when they crossover. People on Earth may have followed a different practical religious theology. However, in the hereafter, the full truth is revealed. They can still go to their places of worship and pray as they prayed on Earth. It is not a matter of you followed this religion, you belong over there. The largest building in the centre of the city is a place where souls can come together and sing praises to God and it has a continuous cycle of thousands of souls, all wanting and waiting to pray, sing and be of service.

"If selfishness starts to arise within and one's thoughts start to show negative emotions, this creates dark spots that show up in their energy field. If they do not strive to remain true, they will have to visit the healers. On most occasions, healing rebalances their soul's energy and the spirit being remains in the land. If this does not work, using one of the teleporter crystals, the 'Law of Attraction' transports the soul to a world that vibrates as they vibrate. Only through being of service, they can work their way back up to a greater Heavenly station. Some souls from the lower regions that caused their light to become dim, try to sneak into the lands above them. Guards monitor every possible entry point, without their attention swerving or shying away from their task. A piercing flame of light will pursue those who try to sneak into the land. Their only way back is through hard work, being of service and loving surrender. They must work to transform their darkened thoughts about the self into light."

They ventured into the city and arrived at a house that had no door, just an open archway where you could walk straight in. Yusif found this strange but then realised that none of the houses had doors that barred your entrance or needed to be opened. If there was a door or barrier, it was a shimmering film of energy and he was told this was only there to keep out the noise and sounds from outside the building. Yusif and the companions passed through the shimmering door and on the other side was someone Yusif instantly recognised; it was his friend Paul. Paul had been a great source of support for Yusif, having a wealth of knowledge that Yusif had used to further his own development. Looking around, Yusif realised the house was full of people he knew. As he looked around, he saw his grandfather standing there, gently smiling.

"You made it," said his grandfather opening his arms. Yusif walked forward and they embraced each other.

"Grandfather, it is so good to see you," said Yusif, with a big smile on his face. "I was hoping that I would see you," said Yusif.

Once they had finished embracing, his grandfather put his hands on Yusif's shoulders and stepped back to leave a space arm's length. He rested his hands on Yusif's shoulders.

"Let me look at you Yusif," said his grandfather. "You are just as I remember you. Come with me, I have a couple I want to introduce you to," said his grandfather.

Yusif's parents from his current birth were sat together awaiting his arrival. It was a welcoming moment for him, as he had not really known them in his current life, due to them passing when he was at such a young age. They explained to Yusif that their passing was predestined, that nothing could be done to change the events and the accident that took their physical lives. They added that they had been watching over him during his Earthly life; they attended every birthday and event that was special to him as he grew up. This made Yusif extremely happy. He wrapped his arms around his parents and grandfather and told them how much he loved them. He thanked them for undertaking their journey to Earth, so that he might be born into the world. During his life on Earth, he had forgotten their faces but now he would have beautiful memories, when he returned to his physical body. He understood that if events had not turned out the way they did, he would not be the person he was today; his life would have taken a different pathway and that each person was on their own spiritual journey. Yusif was aware that families and their members change according to the needs of the soul. Yusif learnt that in one life, you could have been enemies. To heal such a rift, God brings you together in love, so that a healing between you might take place. Births are but a means of entering the world to gain experiences, to aid the soul's growth and development.

Each of the people at the gathering greeted him and to some of them he spoke. It was a happy time for Yusif, as he chatted with those he had not seen for a long time in Earth years, yet in the hereafter, it seemed like it was yesterday. After a while, Yusif felt it was time to leave. After saying his farewells, he re-joined his companions who were waiting outside.

His friend, Paul, joined them, as they visited a few other places in the city. At one house, on being greeted by the host, he smiled, opened his arms and gave Dorcas a deep and meaningful hug. He had not seen her for many years. On Earth, she was one of his close friends who had helped him during his time at school. Her advice kept him out of trouble and helped him turn his life around. Some of his school years had not been pleasant and certainly not the best days of his life. It had been many years since he had seen her and hadn't known that she had passed over and was now in spirit. Seeing Dorcas again, after so many years, brought back memories of her brave and hard-working mother, Hilda, who had been a single parent, working at the hospital and bringing up a family on her own.

Yusif was shown into a room where he took a seat. He was invited to give a short talk to a group that had gathered. He stood up and made his way to the front and sat in the chair so they could all see him. At first, he was a little nervous and was not sure what he was going to say, so he closed his eyes, took a deep breath and cleared his mind. He recited a prayer and as he opened his eyes, a number of thoughts entered his mind. He started to speak as the words came to him and got into a more confident flow. Before he knew it, a good hour had passed, so he started to bring the oration to a close, using the final part of the talk to explain the following:

"The conditions under which people live on Earth happen for a reason. Those that listen to the small voice of guidance, have the best chance of elevating their soul. Those on Earth are bombarded with so much information, it distracts them from what is really important. Some of the things people accept as true about the life of the world, in later years, created nothing more than a state of confusion about what to believe. Try your best to not be swayed by delusions of grandeur. Try to make meditation a part of your daily routine. It helps you keep open the connection to the hereafter. By raising your consciousness and seeing the existence of the world of the hereafter, you will recognise the true spiritual pathway. Each soul is sent inspiration to help them on their journey. You will be inspired to follow the pathway that will lead you to your true centre. Always try to understand the experience and the lessons. The answers will be there if you pay attention and look. Becoming transfixed by the illusion makes it hard to see beyond what it has to offer. There is always a greater reason behind what you see taking place. God does not allow anything to manifest that is not for the greater good of all. Those who meditate and strive will be granted insights and mystical knowledge. This wisdom will give them an understanding that will allow them to expand their conscious awareness. As they raise their consciousness, they will recognise true divine guidance from falsehood. Through their mind's eye, they will be shown signs within their soul. They will see those who reside on high within a clear light. To reach out and see that which is on high, focus and concentrate. Thank you," said Yusif, as he brought his hands together and placed them on his knees.

As the words of wisdom flowed from his mouth, Yusif even learnt a number of things himself. He spent a little more time with Dorcas before it was time for him to leave. Paul, the companions and he left the house and made they their way back through the streets of Bakka. Yusif thanked Paul for such wonderful hospitality, he was so pleased to have met some of his old friends. Once they had said their final goodbyes, Yusif and his companions left the city and headed back to the beach. As they made their return to the beach, the rocks began to change back into crystals and the rainbow on the lake began to reappear.

SPIRITS OF THE LAKE

B ack on the beach, Yusif started thinking about the island that needed restoring. He wondered whether there was any way he could help with the task of recovering the crystals, the Crilarian had spoken about. One of the companions stepped forward.

"Would you like to be of service in the recovery of the crystals and the restoration of an island?"

"Yes, how can I help?" replied Yusif.

"You must visit the island where the lost souls have gathered. For our part, we will use some of the free energy, sound and light sent out by those on the Earth, to help you," said one of the companions.

This was the first time the mention of lost souls had been made and Yusif was puzzled as to how they had become lost and why they were congregated on this island on the lake. He didn't voice his questions, as he remembered that his companions intuitively knew what he was thinking and they usually answered his questions, in time. So, he stood looking out over the lake, wondering how he was going to cross and how he, a mere mortal, was supposed to be of service in recovering the crystal and restoring the island.

A crystal was produced and they told Yusif to look into it. An image began to appear of a stadium, where a football match was being played, again infusing Yusif with confusion, not understanding how this image could possibly be related to his journey or the tasks he had volunteered to undertake. He continued to stare into the crystal and noted that above the pitch, a group of spiritual beings waited. As one team scored a goal, there was an eruption of joy from the crowd and Yusif noticed how this joy generated a huge amount of spiritual energy, which then hovered between the stadium and the observing spiritual beings. These beings gathered up the free spiritual energy and proceeded to redistribute it. Some of it was sent to the hospital and spread among the sick patients, some was used to help balance and heal the Earth; it was used where it was needed the most. The image faded, Yusif and his companions sat down on the beach and the conversation between his spiritual friends resumed.

"There is an island that emerged out of the lake. It was a beautiful place to live, however, a darkness has grown over the island. As for the journey to this place, you must make it alone," said his companion. They did not tell him anymore about the island.

"If you decide to go, you will need to take something with you. Go over to that tree stump with the hole in it," instructed the companion.

Yusif looked over in the direction they suggested. Sure enough, there was the tree stump. It stood about three feet high and about half way up the trunk was a circular hole, which puzzled him for a moment.

Why had he not noticed the stump before? Yusif thought to himself.

"There you must pray. When you have finished, place your hand inside and bring out what you find. What you bring out will determine if you are ready for the task," said the companion.

It was at this point Yusif explained that he had already had a vision about an island that seemed very similar to the one they were sending him to. Although the visions were a little fragmented over a period of time, the last vision he had seen was fuller, however, he did not know the meaning behind it. Ever since having the visions about the island and speaking to the Crilarian, he had wondered whether this was the same island, he had seen during his meditations. They listened as he explained the vision that he'd had last week but said nothing in return.

Walking over to the tree trunk, Yusif sat down to pray as instructed. When he had finished praying, he put his right hand in the hole and reached down. Feeling around inside, he brought out a crystal, a beautifully clear crystal. Swirling around within it were all the colours of the rainbow. As he held it, he could feel it tingling with energy. He re-joined his waiting companions, one of whom handed him a bag, gesturing for him to place the crystal in it.

"Take it with you when you go to the island. This crystal has been gifted to you by the one who creates as He wills. You will know what to do with it when you reach your destination, for we have no knowledge, except that which God reveals to us," said the companion.

Yusif took the bag and carefully placed the crystal within it. He then looped the strap over his head and let it drop onto his shoulder so that the bag hung down to his side.

"When you have a physical body, the laws of service that we must follow, do not apply to you in the same way. Those who find their way from the Earth to our world, retain certain freedoms and options that we do not have. This is why we must leave you to complete the task on your own," said the companion.

"Why is that?" asked Yusif.

"When you took on a physical body, to live as a mortal on Earth, you entered into a world of limitations, however, you were also granted the freedom of choice. Through this you can make your own decisions, be that a choice of being of service or turning it aside. Those who strive to be of service, do so for the good of their own soul. Changes to a soul's condition may take a long time in our world, but that same change can be achieved in a few days or months, while you live on Earth. This is why life on Earth is a special gift which should be treasured and not wasted," said the companion.

"No wonder so many souls want to come to live on Earth," said Yusif.

With the crystal in the bag, Yusif readied himself for the trip to the island. Two of his companions drew close and held him by the arms.

"Are you ready?" asked the companion.

"Yes, I am ready," Yusif confirmed.

Without warning, they all began to rise from the ground and

once they were hovering a few meters high, they were soon on their way to the island, floating across the lake. At first Yusif struggled to find his balance but soon settled down, steadied by his companions. As they made their way across the lake, the water was beautifully clear and blue but deep, yet Yusif could still see the bottom. He could see the sand beds and the scattered rock crystals that sat on the bottom. He noticed there were beautiful but strange creatures swimming through the water, tending to different crystals. Looking at the crystals through the water, they appeared to be very light blue in colour, almost the same shade as the water itself.

If we were travelling any faster, I would not have seen the crystals against the backdrop of the lake, Yusif thought to himself.

As though the companions had heard his thought, their flight slowed down slightly, so Yusif could get a better look as they floated across the lake. There were both singular and clusters of these crystals scattered about on the bed of the lake. A few of them had a much deeper blue colour than some of the others and the companions told Yusif that the crystals in the lake were for the planet Zamzam.

"The strange creatures you see are water spirits. They call themselves Zamureons. They look after the crystals that are here in the lake," said the companion.

Yusif could see that some of the crystals were filled with light, while others appeared like hanging orbs, suspended between the sandy bottom and the surface, moving in a swaying motion like bulbous seaweed. The Zamureons would move the crystals around the lake. This was to recharge the orbs using the sun's light and energy. A little further on, the bed of the lake started to change and become more like a rockery. As the rockery grew and became taller, Yusif could see holes in the rocks. In and out of these caverns, water spirits would come and go. As he watched, he could see a line of Zamureons carrying the light-coloured crystal orbs through the water.

"The water spirits carry some of the crystals to the shoreline of the beach where they place them inside specially designed crystal boxes that are submerged below the water line. This makes it possible for the

Zamureons to put their crystals in the boxes ready for transportation. Keeping them submerged allows the essences within the crystal orbs to remain intact. Once the boxes are full, the custodians from the crystal cave lift the boxes from the lake, seal them, put them on trollies, and push them to the processing chamber in the crystal cave. The custodians also leave boxes filled with depleted crystals from the planet Zamzam for the Zamureons to collect. They had served their purpose and were returned to Bakka to be recharged and taken back to the planet Zamzam," explained the companion.

The companion went on to describe the slightly different process required for the Zamureon crystals, which were obviously required for an aquatic world, explaining that the custodian would move the crystal- and water-filled boxes to the cavern in the processing area, where there was a thirty-foot-deep hole in the floor, which was about three quarters filled with water. At the bottom of the water-filled chamber was a large, crystal-singing bowl fastened to the floor, beside which there was a specialised teleporter crystal, held in place by a mechanical device.

The custodians would remove the box lids and lower the boxes into the water-filled chamber, where the Zamureons working with the crystals would manipulate the water, creating tiny swirling whirlpools just underneath each crystal, that would lift the crystals from the boxes and carry them over to the crystal-singing bowl, one at a time. Once the box from the lake was empty it would be pulled out of the water filled chamber by the custodians.

Once the singing bowl was full, the teleporter crystal was moved into position above them. A slab of crystal would also be lowered to cover the hole in the floor through which the crystal boxes were lowered, in order to contain the vibrations of energy from the crystal bowl and teleporter crystal, during activation. Two Zamureons would each take up a crystal wand, resting them on the outer rim of the bowl. Directly opposite each other, the Zamureons would then start to swim around the bowl in an anti-clockwise direction, ensuring the wands maintained contact with the bowl, speeding up their revolutions until the bowl started to emit a resonant and sustained sound; a deep and rich hum of vibrations. Once the bowl had reached the optimum frequency, the swimming Zamureons maintained that exact pace while the correct pulsations of energy triggered the teleportation crystal to activate, sending the crystals and the Zamureons through a wormhole to their planet Zamzam.

Wow, that would be quite some spectacle to see, thought Yusif and again, the companion (as if reading his mind) began to describe what an observer would see as the process took place.

"As the Zamureons swim at speed around the bowl it causes the water above them to form a whirlpool or vortex, narrow at the bottom, closest to the bowl and wider at the top, closest to the crystal slab. The water would glow in many different colours as the vibrational sound, energy and light from the singing bowl expands, looking very similar to the rainbow on the lake. When the crystal bowl has produced specific colour combinations, it triggers the teleporter crystal to activate, filling with the same colours seen in the water. After the transportation, the water returns to a placid state, the singing bowl is empty, the teleportation crystal moves back into its original position and the crystal slab is removed from the top of the chamber, ready for the next batch of lake crystals. The only other time the slab of crystal was replaced was when the Zamureons were returning with energy-depleted crystals from their world, to be taken into the lake to be recharged with energy. The guards standing by the water chamber would let the custodians know that the slab needs to be placed over the hole."

"Truly amazing!" Yusif uttered quietly.

"If you were to look at their world using your spiritual vision, it would appear like a droplet of water, suspended in time and space. From our world, Zamzam appears to be light blue in colour. Unfortunately, they cannot create the kind of crystals they need in their world, so they have to come to a world that has the right mixture and density of land, water, crystal compounds and minerals, only found in Bakka. Eventually, Zamzam will be transformed; the new will split from the old and move to a higher dimension, carrying with it all those who are ready to move on to the higher vibrating world.

Those left behind on the old world will remain behind for a while; they will need to continue working on and developing themselves, paying attention to their experiences and learning in order to raise their consciousness. They can then start to connect with those who reside in the 'new world'. Those who ascend when their planet transcends, will be tasked with helping those on their 'old world'; those who had fallen below the dividing line that separates the darkness from the light."

"Zamzam is so different from Earth and Bakka, isn't it?" Yusif asked.

"Would you like to know more about Zamzam, Yusif?" asked the companion.

"Oh, yes please! I am always eager to expand my knowledge, experience and awareness companion, thank you," replied Yusif.

"I understand and appreciate your interest," said the companion, "so I will continue, as we have some time before we reach the shores of the island. Zamzam is home not only to the Zamureons, but also to the Mureons, who are a much darker blue in colour to the Zamureons. The Mureons that detect the Zamureons hide when they detect the beautiful, clear, light-blue Zamureons swimming through the water. To elaborate, you need to understand the differences between the Zamureons and the Mureons. Although the words Zamureon and Mureon are similar, when translated in your language, it is like describing spiritual and physical beings, Mureon is the name given to those Zamureons who are not spiritually aware, who do not yet understand or not able to transcend the barrier between their light and the darkness. They have been allowed to come here and play their part in the grand design for that world. In their minds, they believe that what they collect belongs to them. They pick out the crystals that need to be recharged and take them to a place where the energy vibrations are lower. They hope that one day they can find out where and how they are charged, and use that energy to ascend in consciousness. On Zamzam, the supply of the charged crystals is valued in the same way that humans on Earth value certain minerals and rocks, such as gold, silver and other precious metals. The darker blue crystals that need recharging do not vibrate like the lighter blue ones, they vibrate at a much lower frequency and their energy is barely detectable. The charged-up crystals are the power source behind all that has been built in their home world and the Mureons believe the source of the crystal's power will bring them enlightenment. They do not have the technology to recharge the crystals. That knowledge has been withheld from them, as they would not know how to use it if it was given to them. All they could do is collect the crystals and hoard them. The lighter blue crystals that the Zamureons work with vibrate at a higher frequency and this makes them invisible to the Mureons.

"The Zamureons live and work in the vibrations that are higher than those of the Mureons, however, there are many Mureons who are now beginning to become aware of the spiritual connection with their brothers and sisters in this higher vibration. Through choice and spiritual practices, they had retained a conscious connection, which kept their awareness to that world open. Unfortunately, a few distortions have crept into their beliefs and they look to the outer world instead of within themselves for the answers. The information that had been given to many of the unaware Mureons, was a mixture of hearsay and conjecture. Among some of the Mureons, the teachings had been twisted and distorted to keep a number of their tribe in positions of high status. Their understanding was based on historical records and hearsay, rather than an understanding through real spiritual experiences. What they should have recognised as a truth, was treated as something evil.

"A certain selection of the Mureons were allowed to come to the station of Bakka as they were beginning to awaken, however, they did not have enough love within them to carry them across the dividing line that separates the darkness from the light. They were separated from the rest to give them a chance to make that change within themselves so they could ascend. They were indecisive about what they believed. They were open enough to know that something was there and some of them received small amounts of mystical knowledge as guidance, but the weight of that which surrounded them, played heavily on their consciousness, restricting their true potential.

"The Mureons felt the presence of the Zamureons, as they came close, but the Mureons would swim away and hide, because of the fear they had been conditioned to believe in. They did not know the energy they detected was that of their own spiritual brothers and sisters. The Zamureons were working behind the scenes, aiding the growth and development of those Mureons who were seeking the truth. In their lower state of consciousness, their beliefs told them that they should fear all contact with their spiritual world. 'What they cannot see they should fear.' Their thoughts, based on their fears, caused a blockage and they refused to try to see beyond what had been told to them by their leaders. The Mureons were unaware of the bigger picture that surrounded them. However, the Zamureons had an awareness that let them know of a greater truth. They were aware that God sees all and his plan encompasses all. They put their trust in the truth and continued with their work, according to the revelations and inspiration sent to them.

"In Bakka, the Mureon's job was part of the gathering, herding and collecting process. They would gather the darker crystals they found and take them to another part of the lake they thought no one knew about. This work kept them distracted, while the Zamureons continued working and preparing for the transformation of their world. Into the Mureon's psyche was placed the urge to collect. This was to keep them busy and give them purpose, while still aiding their development. So, the Mureons kept collecting and storing the crystals. They did not know it themselves, but their lives and job was still within the limits set by God. The crystals they collected were being taken by the Zamureons to be recharged and the Mureons could not fathom out where the crystals they had gathered, were disappearing.

"The Zamureons knew that their world was being prepared to make a transition. When the planet Zamzam transcends, many of the Mureons that had slipped below the dividing line would be swept away by a wave of energy. They would be taken to a place where they would have to wait to return to their old world. On returning, they would continue with their growth and development from where they left off. They are returned to the base matter that they had accumulated before they were swept away. Some of those that remained on Zamzam, did so because they were between those who transcended and those who were swept away.

"The Zamureons who escape the darkness and transcended would return to become the guides and guardian angels of those living and those waiting to return to the old world. Those who returned to a life on Zamzam, would have their memory of the hereafter removed, until a time appointed. Some of the Zamureons that returned in later times would continue developing and striving to raise their consciousness to even greater heights. Their planet's transcendence would become a tale of the past that the Zamureons would teach the Mureons in the future, in the hope that they remembered something of the event. Their prophets and enlightened ones, who incarnate into their world, would have access to the old records from their past. Within the stories they taught on their return about their past, would be wisdom and guidance, which would help those who were ready to elevate their consciousness," explained Yusif's companions.

"It all sounds very complex, but I can see why that is the case; some beings are just not ready to transcend and need further guidance and spiritual enlightenment. Some of the stories in *The Quran* speak of events that happened on other worlds," mused Yusif.

"Yes," said the companion, "and this process is the same for each planet. All events have a beginning and an end. Even on Earth, those who have passed away, return to help with the evolution of the Earth and its inhabitants. Inspiration is sent to each soul and should they choose to listen, they will ascend in their consciousness awareness and find their way to the Heavenly abode. Through striving, they connect to the higher states of consciousness, from where they receive divine guidance. This divine guidance is beyond the reach of those who turn away from their truth."

THE CRYSTAL STRUCTURES
ON THE LAKE

As they continued their journey across the lake, they began to pass through pulsating waves of energy that were coming from the direction of the rainbow. Yusif began to mentally prepare himself for the remainder of the journey to the island but was suddenly manoeuvred in a different direction… towards the rainbow on the lake.

"Before you visit the island of lost souls, we want you to visit the crystal structure. It will be good for you to have a look around and know more about the kind of work that goes on in this land," said one of the companions.

Once they had passed through the rainbow, Yusif could see three pyramids. The largest structure was divided into three sections, like one pyramid sitting on top of the other. It looked similar to when a child draws a picture of a Christmas tree; each graduation overlapped the other and only the top section looked as though it came to a point. He intuitively knew that the two smaller structures were places where souls could go to learn and train as part of their development.

Two walkways from the largest structure connected to the two smaller ones and there was a narrower walkway connecting the two smaller pyramids. The walkways were like having fifteen lanes of highway, stretching between the two buildings. They did not have any fences or walls to stop someone falling over the edge, although because of the size of the walkways, there was no real need to walk too close to the edge. There were a number of pillars under the walkways that supported their weight and kept them steady. Looking closer, he could see energy moving along the walkways and through the supporting pillars, bi-directionally, moving all the way down and into the lake waters, energising it and keeping it purified.

Yusif was shown in his mind's eye how the pillars extended into the water and rested on the rocky bed of the lake. It was in the caves below the pillars where the Zamureons stored many of their crystalline orbs. Some of the cave entrances were directly below the crystal structure. At the cave's entrance, Yusif saw the Zamureons coming and going from tunnels that ran all the way to the underwater caverns under the structures. Here the crystals would be stored for a while, as they received energy alignment from the crystal structure before they were taken into the lake to receive a final energy boost.

Above the waterline, the base section of the large structure was more solid than the sections above. Inside the base walls of the crystal structures themselves, numerous colours swirled around, however, the colours in the base structure were bold and deep as they moved. The middle section was made of a finer, more transparent crystal and had similar colours but they were lighter and brighter; more radiant. The top crystal section was finer still, with very bright and lustrous swirling colours. The top of the structure was not a point (as it appeared to be from a distance) and unlike the other two smaller crystal structures, it levelled off and had a flat surface. On this flat roof were seven large crystalline orbs. They were positioned to touch the outer edges of the platform and had a couple of rods of crystal between each orb, connecting the crystalline orbs together and creating an enclosure at the top of the structure. Each of the crystalline orbs was one of the colours of the rainbow and it was the energy released through them that created the aura, which surrounded the crystal structures.

A central pillar extended above the flat roof, almost level with the top of the crystalline orbs. Extending from the central pillar and running across the roof, seven crystal wands carried energy to the seven crystalline orbs and at the apex of the pillar, rested a one-inch slab of white, transparent crystal, which was connected to seven smaller crystal wands. The companion explained that the energy would flow through the wands to the tray and that once the final part of the quest on the island was completed, there would materialise a new crystal upon the tray.

His companions told him that others had made numerous attempts to complete the task, but they did not have the depth of spirit needed to succeed. They had to be rescued from the island and when they were found, they were drained of energy and had to spend some time in the healing sanctuary, restoring and rebalancing their energy levels. They were given a grand reward for trying. No one fails; they were just not quite ready for such a quest. It was their willingness to be of service for the greater good of all, that was appreciated by God. For this God grants rewards. They were permitted to try, as part of their own development, learning a great deal about themselves during the experience.

As they got closer to the base of the crystal structure, Yusif looked up. The crystal structure was so high, the top seemed to disappear. They entered the structure via an opening about a quarter of the way up the crystal structure and made their way through a number of corridors carved into the base, which eventually opened up into a room that had a hole in the floor, just like in the crystal cave on the beach. Yusif smiled, as he knew he was going to get another chance to float down to a lower level.

They stepped over the edge and floated down to enter a large cavern, bigger than the public parks in Yusif's home town and strangely, although he knew he was inside, he felt like he was outside, as there were trees that created a woodland area, surrounded by footpaths, along which souls could walk, with benches spaced at regular intervals, for them to rest or just take in the vista before them. There was also grassland where souls could relax, a playground for children and a pond, in which there were different kinds of fish swimming. In the middle of this place, was a large central pillar, like a tower, reaching all the way up to the roof, as though it was holding it up, with its base seeming to go down through the bottom of the cavern, where it rested on the bottom of the lake bed. There were different coloured streams of energy running up and down the pillar and along the floor of the cavern, down into the water.

There were pools of all different sizes that contained healing waters, where souls would come to heal and rebalance their energies. Yusif could see that the energy swirling around in the base centre was continuously revitalising the water in the pools that souls were relaxing in. There were cubicles and a hut; even houses, large and small, where souls could spend time together. Most fascinating was the waterfall, where souls could sit under the cascading water, letting it wash over them. Yusif could see dark energy washing away from some of the souls, as the water streamed over their bodies, where it would flow away to be neutralised by the pure energy of the water.

"Some of the souls here are from Earth," said the companion. "Humans have found many ways for their souls or consciousnesses to visit this domain, specifically for healing. They come here during their sleeping hours to bathe in the healing pools. You can spot these ones by the languid ways in which they move. The length of time they spend here depends on how deeply they sleep, and the depth of healing required. There are those who are currently sitting in meditation (similar to you, Yusif) however, they are using visualisation meditation, so only their projected consciousness is here. Their visits are transient in nature, only staying for a quick dip in the healing pools. There was also contact made with departed loved ones and spiritual guides, before they returned to their bodies on Earth. Their appearance is much more transparent than those visiting us during sleep, or those whose souls were aware that they have journeyed to this place. There are some who are more adept during their visualisation meditation and they can hold their consciousness here in a steadier manner and for longer periods of time."

"I see what you mean about the transparency and how quickly they flit in and back out of the healing pools, like a flicker or faint glimmer before returning to their bodies. It is fun to watch." Yusif said.

"It is," agreed the companion, "it is promising to see so many coming to be cleansed and healed, trying to become better and closer to God. There are also souls that come here to meet their guardian angels. They might chat for a while, with their guardian angels passing on messages of guidance to them, or talking about upcoming experiences they had agreed to go through, as well as planning new ventures and gaining an understanding about their experiences. Their manifestation here is more solid, just like yours. If you look closely, you can see the cord that tethers their souls to their bodies too."

"Interesting," Yusif mused, "so, will I get to be cleansed, healed or meet my guardian angel? He asked.

"Would you like to try out the healing pool, Yusif? It may help to prepare you for your quest," the companion asked.

"Oh yes please," replied Yusif.

"OK, choose a pool and slide into it. When you feel fully reinvigorated, step out and we'll continue our journey. While you are in the pool, I will continue to explain more about our other visitors," instructed the companion.

Yusif and his companions slipped into the pool fully clothed. It looked and felt like water as it pressed against his spiritual body, a gentle tingling making him shudder as the water swirled around him. He immediately felt a warmth and wellbeing suffuse his body and mind, thinking he would like to stay in the pool forever.

The companion continued to teach Yusif about the visitors they had to this plane:

"Souls that have passed over can come here to meet those from Earth who were struggling with issues. Even pets can come here to meet those who they used to live with on Earth, to let them know that they are still alive. This whole place was set up to be of service to others that they might heal and restore their soul's energy."

Yusif opened his eyes and turned around in the pool, taking in all the unfamiliar wonders the cave had to offer. This place was like a small world all on its own. "What is that shimmering veil section over there used for?" asked Yusif.

"Ah, that is the place of dreams. Inside that veil, souls can manifest anything that they want. For those who do not have much of what the Earth has to offer, they are allowed to manifest all that they desire. Each one of us has dreams of what we would like. This is where those dreams are allowed to manifest. There are rules surrounding what it is they can manifest. Certain creations of their base matter, or self, are not permitted. Those that do try to manifest such desires are immediately transported to the lower regions. This place is for the manifesting of material things, such as houses, money, gold and other riches. When such manifestations are created, they are only a temporary condition. It is a place where the soul is able to let go; it is a place of final release from the need to have such things while on Earth. Their manifestations encapsulate them in a small whirlwind of energy. The darker the whirlwind the greater the soul's desire to hold onto what they manifest. However, those who are on the inside of the whirlwind, perceive it as a place that is real. Every direction that they look forms some aspect of the vision to create a world. They are surrounded by delusions of grandeur," continued the companion.

Yusif and his companions stepped out of the pool, they all felt refreshed and energised, their clothing immediately feeling dry as the unneeded energy gathered into a ball and as if by magic, it floated through the air back into the pool. They continued with their 'tour'. After walking around for a while, they went into a different cavern, where there was row upon row of strange machines, manned by several souls. After watching the production line, Yusif realised that the machines made the outer cases for the crystalline orbs, the other row was for what went inside them.

Yusif and his companions made their way to the beginning of the process, which started with bags of the granulated crystals that had been crushed in the crystal cave. A bag of the crystal particles was poured into a hop-like container above the machine, where a scoop full was taken and placed into a smaller container below and carried along on a conveyor belt, to a heating element, which caused the contents to liquify. The glue-like liquid was moulded into seven-inch spheres (similar to glass blowing) and moved along to the next stage.

The new crystalline orb was then injected, via a heated needle, with a mixture of powdered crystal and a specialised liquid, some of the energised lake water, which triggered the crystalline orb to expand to the required circumference. The newly-created crystalline orb was lowered into a conduit of the energised water, which partially activated the internal mixture and carried them away, bobbing along, to the chamber underneath the crystal structure, to be collected by the Zamureons and taken to a place where they would be stored.

Beneath the cavern where Yusif and his companions stood, you could look down and see the bottom of the lake as well as the caverns where the Zamureons had gathered their crystals. There were piles of them covering the bed of the lake. The pulses from the crystal structure energised the water in the cavern and this fully activated the Zamureon crystals. Finally, the Zamureons gathered them up and took them to the boxes by the lake shore, to be transported to the planet Zamzam. Depending on what the crystals were used for would depended on how long they remain charging in the lake.

After watching how the crystalline orbs were made, the group made their way back to the open space, where many souls continued to enjoy relaxing and healing. They continued on to the exit, moving up through a hole in the ceiling, which took them to another room where there was a stream of energy that lifted them up to the next level. They walked past rooms where souls were sat at desks, facing a teacher who was explaining the virtues of life and of how being of service was the greatest gift you could give.

They continued upwards, reaching the second section of the crystal structure and Yusif discovered that this was where all the artists came to learn and enhanced their creative skills. There were all kinds of artists expressing themselves through a variety of media, including voice, painting style, writing, experimenting and ethereal movement. This was the place where some of the most talented souls would study before going to Earth. Some of them would become the inventors and innovators who would inspire a generation of souls on Earth. As they walked along the corridor, they passed many people, in rooms where they were playing musical instruments. It was so nice and to hear music so beautifully played, understanding how its power could stimulate and amplify emotions, trigger memories, enhance a person's mood and well-being; create a sense of unity and connection, to inspire motivation. There was also a room where experimental sounds were being created and tested. The companions took Yusif to a room where he was greeted by a wonderful soul called Earl.

EARL'S MUSIC STUDIO

E arl was divinely inspired to create much of the music that
filled Bakka. He took them to a room where there were all
kinds of musical instruments. All the music created was to
help restore that which had fallen out of harmony and balance. On
one side of the wall were hundreds of small crystal orbs containing
different types of music. The music stored within these crystal orbs
were to help with the restoration of souls. Music was composed
using lights, vibrations, sounds and frequencies. They were blended
together into tunes that created harmonious vibrations, which could
restore the more disruptive vibrational energy. Some music was taken
and used in both the lower and higher realms, others were collected
and taken to the city of Bakka, for use by its residents. Each crystal
and crystalline orb (for the Zamureons) had been specifically and
musically enhanced to treat every kind of condition.

Earl began to speak and even his words sounded as though he was
singing them. Earl explained the nature of music, its composition,
purpose and effects:

"Each soul is unique. They may look similar but there are subtle
differences in their vibrations, frequencies and alignments. It is a
little bit like an octave – you can play a low note and you can play the
same note at a higher pitch. Each note vibrates at a different rate and
frequency, or tempo where lower is slower and higher is quicker. Each
note has either base- or treble-dominant pitch vibrations within it,

to give it its expression," said Earl, as he gesticulated with his hands to the melody of his words.

Earl explained that when he composes music, he becomes the music. He was able to examine or probe the music and manipulate the frequencies within each note.

"Imagine you were a drop of water on the leaf of a tree. Beneath you, a stream flows by. You fall off the leaf and into the stream. I am like the drop and the stream is the music. When dropping into the stream, you become the stream. Music vibrations are everywhere. It is a matter of tuning in," Earl explained, as he walked over to a chair next to the piano, beckoning them to follow.

They all walked over to stand by Earl and the piano. Earl reached out his hands, passing them over Yusif's body without physically touching him, as though he was trying to sense something from Yusif's aura. It only took a few seconds for him to scan Yusif in this way, becoming attuned to, and gaining knowledge of Yusif's soul frequency. Earl sat down at the piano and instructed Yusif to sit down with him and close his eyes.

Yusif sat in the seat next to Earl and closed his eyes, while his companions stood behind them. Earl picked up a guitar and started to play. Immediately, Yusif felt a tingling ripple throughout his spirit body. Then Earl stopped playing and lifted the piano lid. He started to play a few notes on the keyboard and this time, Yusif felt the music penetrate his inner most self.

"That's incredible," said Yusif.

The music's vibrations flowed over Yusif like a wave, followed by tiny ripples of energy that made their way from his head to his toes. Yusif felt revitalised after a few moments, just like the healing pool, however, with his eyes still closed, his vision filled with beautiful patterns moving and changing as the chords and notes changed. Yusif could see with his mind's eye that the room became filled with harmonious bubbles of light. They were everywhere, lights coming and going and flying around the room. Once Earl stopped playing, the lights faded and then Yusif opened his eyes.

"It's the ability to influence the vibrations of the notes as they flow through you, time and space, that results in the healing and balancing you feel. One single note contains the frequencies of every other note. It is a matter of looking inside the note, which allows one to then influence all the different frequencies within that note, to harmonise it with the exact frequency of the spiritual being or situation you are working with. All this can be done in a split second. Just as you learn to think on multiple levels, rather than one level, you can also learn to listen to a chord of music and within yourself, you can hear each note individually or all at the same time. Sounds are so powerful. Music is different sounds put together to create a tune. Some are more beautifully and intricately created than others," Earl clarified.

Earl then took them to adjoining rooms used for healing through sound.

"Souls come here to relax and realign their energy. Did you notice the small crystals and crystalline orbs on the wall, in the corridor leading to the healing rooms? Each of them has thousands of sounds and tunes stored within them. When a soul needs healing, they choose the one crystal they are drawn to and place it into a small holder next to a crystal bed. The soul will lay down on the bed, place an adjustable headset connected to two wands, over their temples and start to relax, as you do when you start a meditation. As they relax, a part of their consciousness connects with the energy from the wands, which are programmed to recognise the soul's true frequency. The frequency is then matched to the sounds or music recorded in the crystal. Through this, they receive the frequencies that they need – to heal, balance and realign their spirit's energy." Earl stated.

"As the music's soothing sounds are heard by the soul, they fall in to a deep, relaxing state, which allows the healing to take place. On a deeper level, a realignment of their spirit's patterning, restores and heals them. It is a little bit like a fingerprint – once you get the exact match, the vibrations in the music realign and heal a soul on so many different levels," continued Earl.

As they walked down the aisles, souls lay on the beds listening to music. Yusif noticed how they would change colour as the music penetrated their inner most being. He could see the way the music was helping rebalance and heal each of them. Some of these beings had returned from working in areas filled with undeveloped beings. They came here to be restored to their former condition. Any irregular attachments or vibrations of lower energy could be seen draining away. This dark energy could be seen flowing from them and going down into a crystal underneath the bed. Once the energy had been gathered, it passed to another crystal, under the bed where it was transformed and completely neutralised.

"The music's soothing affect is an important part in the healing process. With sound, there are vibrations and with vibrations, there is the production of energy. Music relaxes the soul and helps speed up the healing process, as it puts the soul into a receptive state of mind to receive. When a mind is closed, it blocks the soul's ability to receive. It is an individual's openness to receive love, trust and truth, which restores the balance. This allows the soul to change the condition of itself to bringing about an elevation in its consciousness," explained Earl.

Yusif pondered for a moment. He was thinking about the next time he gets out his own guitar, he will think about what Earl explained about music, as he entertains himself.

"Thank you, Earl," said Yusif.

Yusif was feeling so enlightened from what Earl had explained to him about music and its benefits.

In the healing rooms, some souls were being used as conduits through which healing energies would flow. These souls would attune themselves to the energies in the higher states of awareness. They would direct that energy through themselves and into the soul under their care. This soul-to-soul healing was another way of getting to the deeply rooted pattering within the soul. Crystal healing was restricted to the crystal being used, meaning that the crystal chosen, the one the soul was most drawn to, had its limitations. Soul-to-soul healing could be adjusted and refined, allowing both the healer and the soul to receive healing.

They moved on to where Earl had a workshop, in which he had been working on a new project.

"Mario gave me a very special singing bowl," Earl excitedly revealed. "It needs two hands to carry it. Mario confessed that he had been inspired to create this singing bowl, he didn't know why, but he felt he had to make one that could hold a lot of energy, once it is activated. This bowl has to hold all seven colours of the rainbow and be able to vibrate with all the frequencies at once. These energies are not just from around Bakka, but from the seven Heavens above. If it had not been for the spirit of inspiration helping from the higher Heavens, the project would have never been completed," explained Earl.

Yusif looked at the bowl. To him it looked like any other kind of singing bowl that he had seen.

Earl asserted that when Mario passed the singing bowl to him, he was inspired to create some of the most powerful sound frequencies of energy that he had ever worked on. He had to develop new techniques, using the inspiration from the higher Heavens, as a means of channelling this energy into the bowl. The seven vibrational frequencies had to align with the energy from the seven Heavens, as well as infusing the symbol sent from each Heaven, into the singing bowl itself. This was to help with the encoding of the energy that would be used when it was fully activated.

Earl admitted he was not sure why the spirit of inspiration had directed him to create such a powerful set of frequencies, all he knew was that he had to. He finished preparing the bowl a short time ago, and it had taken him some time to learn how to channel the energy frequencies from the higher heavens so that they flowed and aligned perfectly into the bowl. Through the challenge of the task, he explained how he had grown and developed during the process. He was waiting for the spirit of inspiration to influence him to test it, to ensure it contained all the right frequencies needed. He told Yusif and his companions that he felt it was his greatest work to date.

They walked past another room which contained a couple of large singing bowls, much larger than the usual hand-held singing bowls.

"These singing bowls are also made out of a very special crystal," said Earl.

Yusif looked into the room and saw that one of the bowls was about five-feet wide and four-feet deep, the other was about half that size. In the centre of each singing bowl was a teleporter crystal, suspended in mid-air, a little above the rim of the bowl. It was kept suspended in the air, by the energy in the room, which was palpable. There was also a crystal wand, attached to a wooden handle, which in turn was attached to a device that could keep the crystal wands turning around the rim of the singing bowls. Only one of the wands was actively turning at this point in time and it was turning at a constant speed, creating a specific sound and energy, which was drawn up into the transporter crystal.

"The energy created by the singing bowls is being transported to the location that was programmed into the teleporter crystal. There is an island that is holding up a number of rock crystal structures, which need to be raised to allow them to maintain their energy and stop it from draining away. Once certain conditions change on the island, the rotation speed of the wand will slow down and bring the floating rocks back down to the ground, while at the same time, the wand on the second, smaller crystal bowl will start to spin. Once both wands reach the same speed, the rocks will have fully descended back down to land. The second bowl, which is stationary at the moment, is aligned to emit a higher frequency, which will cause the outer rock, around the floating crystal structures, to break. Once the island becomes repopulated, its inhabitants will live and work in these large crystal structures," explained Earl.

Yusif tried to enter the room for a better look but a vibration of energy in front of the entrance blocked his way.

"No one is allowed to enter the room as it will disturb the energy and the person would be sucked into the teleporter crystal and find themselves on the island. Any disturbance to the energy would also cause the rocks to fall out of the sky," warned Earl, as he reached out to check there were no leaks around the shimmering door, which would allow energy to escape.

With the tour of Earl's studio compete, it was time for Yusif and his companions to leave. Before they said their goodbyes, Earl gave Yusif a small bag containing seven crystal orbs.

"These are for you. Each orb vibrates at one of the notes of the scale. You will need them on your journey. Each crystal orb holds one of seven sacred symbols, which you will have to figure out how to use them, when you reach the island," said Earl, as he handed the bag to Yusif.

"Thank you, Earl, it has been a real pleasure. I will keep in mind all that you have told me," said Yusif.

He put the bag of crystal orbs in the first bag he was given by his companions. They said their goodbyes to Earl and left the studio.

"That was so interesting," Yusif said to his companions, as they walked down a corridor.

They went up to another floor in the second section, where there was only a single, large room. It was filled with thousands of souls, all sat in meditation. As Yusif watched them meditating, striving and pursuing their path, which would allow them to ascend to the next dimension, he also noted that there seemed to be a continuous rotation of souls entering and leaving the room, as well as streams of energy flowing from the souls and being channelled towards the central pillar. It was in the base of the crystal structure that Yusif had first seen this pillar that ran from the base, up through all the levels of the crystal structure, to the roof.

Yusif eyes scanned upward along the pillar to the ceiling, where he saw the most amazing and intricate pattern of concentric ripples radiating outward to the edges of the ceiling, in ever increasing sizes as they went, to finally connect to forty-eight crystals on the outermost edge. Connecting the pillar to the innermost concentric ripple, were seven crystal wands which distributed the energy gathered from the meditating souls, across and around the central pillar, to be continuously transferred to the adjacent larger concentric ripples, all the way to the outer edge of the ceiling. As the number of concentric ripples increased, so did the crystal wands connecting each concentric layer. Yusif realised that the seven wands represented a note on the musical scale and that as the number of wands increased across the ceiling, so the musical notes also changed into the semitones of the previous musical note. As the energy passed through the ceiling it created the beautiful rainbow effect that could be seen all around the crystal structure. The generated energy also created small pulsations that could be felt by Yusif and his companions as they approached the central structure. It really made Yusif happy to see so many souls sat in meditation. In the physical world most meditation was done alone or in small groups. In the afterlife, there were thousands that would sit in large groups expressing and sending out from themselves, loving energy.

THE PLANET ZAMZAM

Aspace became available in the room where many souls were meditating and Yusif was invited to sit with them and meditate. Yusif sat and closed his eyes and within a few moments, he felt himself rising up out of his body, just like he had at home, only much quicker. He stood by the side of his sitting spiritual body, looking down upon himself, thinking, *this is strange, I'm already in spirit form in this spiritual world, how can I be here again?*

"You have more than one spiritual body, Yusif" said a female voice, from behind him.

Yusif turned and saw a beautiful being, hovering a few meters away, floating above those sat in meditation. She introduced herself as Sara, a companion of Paul. She beckoned Yusif to follow her and as he moved forward, he too rose above those who were sat in meditation.

"The body you are now in is of a higher vibration. It is much finer and will allow you to visit places your other bodies are too dense to visit," said Sara, as he moved closer to her.

"Yes, I remember. We have seven bodies that I am aware of, starting with the physical," replied Yusif.

"That is correct," Sara confirmed. "I am here to take you on a short journey. Would you like to visit the planet Zamzam?" Sara asked.

"Yes, it would be an honour," replied Yusif, feeling both excited and wary at the same time.

Moving to this higher vibration of energy, allowed them to travel with great speed and it did not take them long to arrive at the planet Zamzam. Initially, they arrived at a point where they had a view of the whole planet and Yusif was surprised to see that it was much larger than he expected, at least double the size of the Earth.

"Before we enter Zamzam, focus on creating a bubble of energy around yourself. We are about to enter the planet's outer atmosphere and the bubble you create will allow you to breathe easier, as we move through their world," instructed Sara.

Sara demonstrated to Yusif how she created her own bubble of energy around herself. She held her hand out in front of her, turned anti-clockwise in a full circle as the energy poured from her hand to create the bubble. She looked at Yusif from within her protective sphere and urged him to replicate the actions for himself. He put out his hand and visualised a bubble of energy encircling him as he turned, however, because this was the first time he had attempted this, his energy was not quite strong enough to create a robust enough sphere to sustain the journey, so Sara moved closer to Yusif and gave him some additional energy, to help create a stronger field.

"Breathe as normal and you will be fine, as we travel through the outer layers of the planet. The Mureons will not be able to see us, unless we wish to be seen, as we are vibrating at a speed higher than they can perceive. We will be traveling to the inner depths of Zamzam. Can you remember when you were in the crystal cave and those there could move up and down the energy to different floors? This is the same kind of process. Think the direction you wish to travel and you will move," Sara explained.

They began to move forward, entering the outer atmosphere, which was a reddish mist. This was followed by an orange mist, then a yellow mist and a green mist. "These mists are remnants of previous vibrational colours that the planet once vibrated at," said Sara, "and as the planet's innermost vibration is currently blue, it results in a more watery planet. Soon it will be making a transformation to indigo."

As they passed through the outer layers of the planet's past states the water changed. It was denser than the other layers. The protective sphere around him started to contract, closing in on Yusif and causing his breathing to become a little erratic. He began to think that the protection around him would not hold much longer but Sara moved closer to him and steadied his energy, as they made their way.

Protected by the energy force around them, they moved, undetected, through the outer structures carved into the planets inner shell. Yusif was now feeling less anxious as his breathing returned to normal and as he passed through objects in his second spiritual body, he realised that he wasn't feeling the denser material pressing against him, not at all like when he first passed through the wooden door in his home. Once through the inner shell of the planet, their protective spheres stabilised, no longer contracting as they had previously and Yusif felt a sense of relief at that. They both paused their journey and turned back to view the blue layer they had just passed through, Yusif realising that there were crystalline structures carved into the layer, but there was no time to explore that element further, as Sara turned back toward the planet and started to make her way down into one of the planet's inner oceans and of course, Yusif followed.

The water was not as dense as the water on Earth and neither did Yusif feel the pressure of the water above him, the deeper they travelled into its fathomless bowels. This could also have had something to do with the different gravitational pull felt on this planet, compared to that of Earth. There was just enough gravity to stop you from floating off in a particular direction, no matter which way you were standing. Their protective shields were no longer required, which allowed them to breathe easier, feeling more relaxed and able to appreciate what he was seeing under the water, watching the Mureons going about their daily lives.

It was a beautiful place. In their normal habitat, there were many different kinds of Mureons, distinguishable by their many and varied body colours and shades, although their main physical body types and facial features remained similar, there were additional details that differentiated them, such as some having small antenna on top of their heads, while others had gills in different areas of their bodies; some had fins that helped them to move quickly through the oceans.

Just like on Earth, the same race (human) of many colours, sizes, styles and cultures, overall though, they had learnt to live in peace with each other. Sara explained that they had been through their troubles and now worked in harmony with their environment and each other; that there was a fair structure in place that allowed them all to have homes, use energy that was free and cycle through many roles and jobs, so each could learn and develop. They were more aware of God and service than humankind was.

As the main outer vibrational colour of the planet was blue, so everything had a hint of blue to it. Yusif learnt that there was a variety of different types of water – some water was lighter with little or no water pressure where some was denser or heavier and each variety of water, exhibited a different shade of blue. This understanding of water was similar to the way the native Inuit or Yupik of Earth, would describe the variance of snow they encounter on a daily basis, which uses forty to fifty words, compared to those who experience snow maybe once or twice a year. On the planet Zamzam, there were also many different words used to name or describe the nature of those varied bodies of water.

As Yusif looked around him, he could see many beautiful buildings and other structures created from crystallised water, or carved into the blue shell surrounding the planet, where the majority of the Mureons lived. With the planet being spherical, just like Earth, the buildings created in the blue shell, appeared to be at angles to one another and because the planet was so large, some of those buildings could house millions of Mureons. The water crystal buildings actually sat on deposits of crystallised water and gave the appearance of floating in mid-air; they hung like lanterns suspended in time and space. With the planet twice as large as Earth, some of the structures were so big, they could each house around one million Mureons. There were hundreds of these cities, housing billions of Mureons.

Some structures were built like towers, where others were low and flat, covering large areas upon which small towns and larger cities had grown. Many of these places were self-sustaining and one could spend their whole life living there and never need to leave.

The deposits of crystallised water were used to build and repair the structures of Zamzam, which were mined directly from the planet's own resources. This was one of the jobs done by many of the Mureons, who lived in the structures carved into the blue shell.

This crystallised water was to those of Zamzam, the same as iron or metal to the inhabitants of Earth. Some of the material could be blended together to create a rubbery substance, which could then be moulded into different shapes. The substance would dissolve back into the water, which meant continuous work was needed to repair the structures. This allowed for greater utility as it was very flexible. One of its many uses was for manufacturing vehicles for transporting Mureons around the planet.

The vehicles used for transport were powered by the crystals sent from Bakka, where the energy contained in them propelled the vehicles through the water. As the vehicles glided, they looked as though they were flying. There were many different models of vehicle, such as single passenger vehicles, right up to train-like conveyances, allowing many passengers to travel throughout the planet. And the most beautiful and awe-inspiring fact about the crystal energy used, was that it did not pollute the atmosphere. In Zamzam, the energy contained within the crystal orbs was the driving force behind many of the inventions that were created. They were used like batteries and plugged into everything that needed a power source. It took only one crystal to fuel a single transportation vehicle, however, some of the larger vehicles had two or three, maybe more crystals, to drive and power them along.

In the same way electricity is used to power many things on Earth, the Mureons used both water and the energised crystals to power their cities. They also invented a way to extract the energy from the water around them and when this was combined with the crystals, they had a power source that could keep their structures constantly running on free energy. They would also use this energy to prevent the cities from moving from their current positions due to the weaker gravitational force of the planet.

The Mureons had learnt to live with and use the environment

and natural resources of their planet. There were large fields that stretched for hundreds of miles, all covered in plant life, their photosynthesis keeping the planet oxygenated. The fields were tended by the Mureons and although some of the fields could cover twelve million kilometres, they were essential to the life of the planet, so they were given a high priority. Some of the fields looked like long pieces of seaweed that reached up to twenty feet in length, swaying from side to side, as though they were being blown in a wind.

Sara and Yusif visited a number of places on the planet Zamzam. The Mureons with whom they visited had found a way to communicate with the Zamureons and other beings in the afterlife. Sara had visited these Mureons before, to give them guidance and instruction. During this whole time, Yusif stayed quiet as he realised the importance of what was going on around him. He thought he should best be an observer during this visit so he could watch, listen and learn, as Sara completed the tasks that had been given to her. Yusif also used this time to reflect on some of the stories he had read in the holy books, back on Earth, as knowing that some of them related to events that took place on other worlds, it would help him to understand the stories in context.

Yusif had met many people on Earth who could communicate with those in the hereafter and realised that Earth must, one day, go through its own transformation and change. The majority of humanity was aware of the holy stories but they paid them little heed. Only those who were ready could understand the importance of the stories and the messages that they conveyed. The Mureons, who were consciously aware, passed the messages on to those who were open to learning and understanding. There were only a select number that would perceive such events for the future and know how to prepare themselves and those around them. These warnings had been foretold in all their holy books and those who were willing to try, could make the necessary changes to their lives. Their message was that there was going to be three sudden surge of energy, like a wave and would be one of the warnings from God, that things were about to change in a major way. This final visit to Zamzam by Sara was to inform them that the change was about to happen and that they should prepare themselves and any others who are aware. Once Sara had delivered the messages to those she had been tasked with visiting, they both left and continued their journey towards the centre of the planet.

As they left the region of the world inhabited and maintained by the Mureons they entered a place where the water was calm and still. Yusif felt it was a strange place, because he felt that he was neither here nor there. They continued on and as they got closer to the centre of the planet, the density of the water around them became lighter. This seemed to be a very quiet place, with not much activity going on and the indigenous beings were sparse. Of the Zamureons Yusif did see, they were stationary, just hanging there alone or in groups, as if they were waiting for something. All Yusif detected about them was that they were waiting to enter the inner sanctuary of Zamzam. They too were in the final moments of their own transformation. There were also Mureons that recognised their calling. They had transcended their worldly life and were about to enter the final purification process. They would then transform to become Zamureons. Soon after passing them, Yusif could see an indigo light in the far distance and as they got closer to the light, they began to encounter many Zamureons that were going about their daily lives. Zamzam had a world within a world. The inner world of Zamzam vibrated on a higher frequency allowing the Zamureons to see Sara and Yusif.

It was not long before they entered another level of the planet, by passing through a number of vibrational pulses and eventually entering into the inner space of the planet. This place was more like Earth where the Zamureons lived on the surface of this inner world. This place vibrated at a much higher frequency than the outer world of the Mureons. Although it was invisible to the Mureons, those that lived here were of like nature. Two beings vibrating at the same rate were solid to each other. If one were to raise their vibrations, they would disappear from the view of the lower vibrating being. This allowed the Zamureons to move around the waters where the Mureons lived, without being seen.

Yusif could see that there were some beautiful buildings, as they headed toward what looked like a large dome sphere that surrounded the city. They entered the dome and made their way toward the centre of the city where there was a large auditorium. Yusif could see millions of Zamureons, sat in rows that circled a stage in the middle, where there was a central stage. Sara motioned for Yusif to join the seated Zamureons in the front row, while she moved to the stage to address all of the beings there. Sara had been tasked with providing the Zamureons with knowledge of the final keys required, that would allow them to begin the transformation, enabling their ascension to their next level of awareness.

Yusif watched with interest as Sara took out a piece of paper Earl had given to her. It detailed an ordered sequence of musical notes that would need to be played at a specific point in the process of transformation and ascension. She used the information to organise the Zamureon musicians, who would play or create the required notes, on the seven giant digeridoos of differing lengths and widths, they were sat behind, in readiness for the music to begin. To the side of the digeridoos were another seven Zamureons, holding crystal wands for striking the singing bowls, again of differing sizes. Sara directed the Zamureons to move to different positions according to the order of the musical notes on the paper. Once they were all in the correct positions, Sara nodded to a Zamureon who also stood at the front and to her left.

Sara spoke for a short time to the multitude of Zamureons in front of her and when she had finished, the Zamureon standing next to her, pulled once on a string of rope, connected to the clapper of a small bell, causing it to produce a single ring. The sound it made was only heard by those who were close by but everyone in the room knew what it meant – it was time to prepare for the coming first of three waves of energy to be sent out.

Each of the Zamureons attending the gathering had their own crystal orb, which they placed on the floor in front of their crossed legs and cupped their hands over. All the crystals in the dome began to glow with a light and as the energy built up in the crystal orbs held by the Zamureons, the energy seeped down into the floor of the dome, making all of the crystal orbs connected. Once they were all connected, the seated Zamureons closed their eyes and prepared for meditation, becoming aware of each other and joining together as one. Sara started to speak to them again, this time taking them all on a guided meditation. As her beautiful voice took them deeper and deeper, the connection between them grew stronger. The energy in the room increased and filled the whole place. When she had finished, the sound of the small bell rang out again; this was the signal for the digeridoo players to ready themselves, awaiting the second ring from the bell, signalling them to start playing. The first digeridoo played had a deep sound to it that resonated in the pit of Yusif's stomach and filled the atmosphere of the auditorium; it permeated the whole place with a low level vibration. This initial sound was followed by the remaining six digeridoos, joining in one at a time, in the order specified by Sara, until all seven digeridoos were playing together, blending into one sound. The energy that had now built up in the room was almost overwhelming, making Yusif feel it was almost impossible to move. It had a profound effect on every soul there. As the sound reached a crescendo, the first wave of energy was released and although initially it was contained within the dome, it suddenly broke through the dome and was released into the wider Zamureon habitat in all directions.

As the Zamureons continued to sit in meditation, pulses of energy continued to ripple through the atmosphere of Zamzam, which created the first wave of separation, allowing the inner planet of Zamzam to shift slightly. Those meditating began to chant in harmony with the overall vibrational sound of the digeridoos and Yusif could sense that they had also started to sway from side to side in unison, as the pulses of energy swirled and moved all around them. The whole atmosphere was now vibrating in harmony to the sound of the digeridoos.

The volume of the Zamureon's chanting began to increase and the sound started to build up, until it reached the level of vibration to create the next wave of energy, which too radiated outward as a pulse.

Having reached the second phase of vibration for the transformation, a new vibration was required, to provide the frequency of sound necessary to continue to the final phase and this was provided by the Zamureons with the crystal singing bowls. Again, one Zamureon started the sound, by spinning the crystal wand around the outer edge of the singing bowl, creating a harmonic mellow overtone which although it resonated at a higher frequency, it blended seamlessly with the deep and rich hum of the digeridoos. As each of the Zamureons took it in turns to activate their singing bowls, the energy in the room increased. When they were all active, everything transformed into a higher state of vibration. This final wave created the separation between the old planet and the new planet of Zamzam. Even Yusif had to focus because of the powerful vibrations that were being created. For a moment, he felt himself begin to transcend and enter another one of this spiritual bodies.

The waves of energy that were sent out affected the whole planet of Zamzam. Even the Mureons stopped what they were doing and looked at each other, not sure what to say or do, as the wave of energy rippled through the atmosphere. They knew of their own spiritual stories but many of them paid little attention to them. However, now these stories were playing out as a reality in their lives. Those Mureons that were spiritually aware of their connection to the Zamureons understood the inner truth behind the rippling effects of the energy around them.

The rippling vibrations of energy allowed the feminine energy of the planet to split from the masculine. The feminine energy began to ascend and move away from the masculine and although it would take a number of years to complete the split, it was now set in motion. The inner planet would now be as a new Heaven for the Mureons that chose to raise their consciousness. Of course, this would not go down well with those who were unaware of their spiritual connection, as the sheer power of the vibrational ripples did cause a few of the buildings to tremble and where structures were weaker, splits zigzagged up the walls. In some places and a number of the floating structures, all the lights went out and the power drained from many of the crystal orbs.

The majority of the buildings managed to survive the energy bursts, but all the Mureons were startled and shaken by what had happened. A lot of work would need to be carried out to repair the structures.

The separation did not totally detach the Zamureons from the planet on which the Mureons live. The Zamureons would be tasked with working to help those who were left behind, becoming their guides and guardian angels from the afterlife. This would be another stage of the journey, to bring the entire population of the Mureons home, to the hereafter.

As the inner world of Zamzam pulled away from the main planet, all that would be left was an image of what was once there. This image would remain for a while, recorded in their eternal record, changing over time to become the colour violet. Eventually the whole of the planet Zamzam would be seen as a violet-coloured planet, as the new essence radiated its inner light. This was the final colour before the final transformation into a white light. The blue colour would eventually be pushed out to become one of the outer rings around the planet, like the other outer rings that Sara and Yusif passed through, when they first entered the atmosphere of Zamzam.

The new souls born on planet Zamzam would become holders of the violet flame of purity. Only those who were spiritually aware would have access to this new inner world of the violet flame. This event had been foretold in the Mureons scriptures thousands of years ago and now that it had come to pass, all the Mureons questioned the current teachings that had been passed down through the ages. It would be their questioning that would be the start of their new age.

With the completion of the task, Sara and Yusif began to make their way back to the world they had left behind. It was now for the Zamureons to complete whatever tasks they needed to do to ensure that the separation and transformation continued to its completion.

Sara and Yusif returned to Bakka and the crystal structure on the lake, back into the room where many souls, including Yusif, were sat in meditation. Yusif was speechless at what he had witnessed and when he looked at Sara, she smiled and nodded her head, knowing that Yusif could not find the words to talk about their journey and experience on Zamzam. Yusif had to give himself a moment before re-entering his spiritual body as what he had experienced and learnt, was beyond anything he might have imagined.

Once Yusif was back in his spiritual body, opened his eyes to find Sara had gone. He looked around to see his companions waiting for him. He left the meditation room and followed them as they explained, even on Earth, those who had passed away, return to help with the evolution of the Earth and its inhabitants.

"Inspiration is sent to each soul. Some souls find their way by paying attention and listening; striving to connect to the hereafter through their higher consciousness. As they do this, they do indeed become wise to the realities of life on Earth. The event you witnessed will become a tale of the ancients in their world. Some of the Zamureons that transcended will incarnate back into a life on Zamzam and teach the Mureons about the stories from their past. Just as there are lower worlds in this part of God's kingdom, many souls are still able to incarnate back on Earth, to experience and learn so that they might grow. This cycle of life happens on every planet, giving those who live there more than one chance to get things right. Within the messages that their teachers bring to them, they will start to learn. In the teaching will be wisdom and guidance to inspire those who were ready."

Yusif accessed his own memories of some of the stories he had been told as a child and as he thought about the stories, inspiration filled in some of the missing information and understanding to complete the picture. The story of Noah made much more sense to him, now he had seen some inspiration about the event. He would refresh himself about the stories in The Quran, when he returned to his physical body on Earth. He learnt that the event had taken place on another world. Such stories were put into the holy books so that those with vision might remember and understand, as inspiration reveals the truth. All that he had learnt up to now, gave him an understanding and insight that allowed him to conclude that, no matter what happens in our world, even the things that are perceived as unthinkable acts, all happen for the betterment of the world. *The life we create is based on our inner choices. Each soul is presented with an opportunity to amend their ways and re-join the path towards their development if they so choose. Their ideas or lack of striving will by no means halt God's plan.* They continued their walk, going up a few floors, exploring different rooms in the second level.

IN THE LIBRARY

N ear the top of the section on the second level, they eventually entered the library of higher learning and wisdom. Beings from all over this quadrant of the galaxy would use this library to study, before setting off to complete their tasks. There were books about the beginning of creation, meditation, healing, music and sound, vibrations, working with energy, herbal medicines, crystals, astronomy and, languages, modern and ancient. There were books about every spiritual topic you would ever want to acquire.

In one corner of the library there were a couple of beings who Yusif recognised as guards. They stood straight in their posture, were covered from head to foot in a protective uniform that had a purple glow to it and the energy that radiated from them, was that of an immovable object. Yusif could feel their strength and purpose, which was like a rod of iron. Yusif looked at them with curiosity, as he had never seen a guard this close up before. They stood there, in front of a shimmering door, with their eyes closed.

"They do not need to use their physical eyes. They see like we see but with closed eyes," said the companion.

"Why do they not use their eyes?" Yusif queried.

"The guards see more with their mind's eye, only using a body in Bakka to let you know they are there. Their method of sight enables them to live in this world and other worlds simultaneously, watching continuously for the approach of anything sinister from those worlds, protecting Bakka from the dimensions of darkness that are in the realms below. They only return to their bodies to allow some beings entry into the rooms behind them. Even when the guards return here, they are able to keep an awareness and do their duty in both worlds," the companion explained.

Why would there be a couple of guards for a library? What is so special about and behind that shimmering door? Yusif thought to himself.

Suddenly, the guards parted as two beings walked past them and through the shimmering door. The guards immediately returned to standing in front of the door again.

"They have full awareness of who is permitted to enter the rooms behind the door and of course, those who don't," the companion said.

"What is behind that shimmering door?" Yusif asked, as he turned to his companions.

"Through that door are the eternal records. Some souls that oversee worldly events on a specific world are able to monitor their progress. They can travel to that world and work to bring about the desired event, in line with God's plan or they can watch how the plan is unfolding and ensure that it is kept on course. It is a little like *Google* maps – you can view places from afar or you can zoom right in and see the smallest of details. Events on these worlds can be seen unfolding in real time," the companion told him.

Yusif knew there were records of deeds, but he did not know too much about them, so this new information was a real help in his understanding about how things work in the hereafter.

"Each world in the hereafter has a library with a room containing record keeping crystals. Every moment is recorded and those who can read, have access to these records through which they gain clarity about a matter. They can see forward, backward or the present. They use the vision to offer guidance to those in need and to those who seek," explained the companion.

"That is truly amazing," said Yusif.

"These specialised crystals keep a recorded account of everything that happens in various worlds within the local solar systems. In each room there are three crystals, one crystal, known as Illyin, records all the good moments and deeds, one, known as Sijjin, records the bad and the third crystal known as hikma, which balances both and is full of wisdom. Through the wisdom crystal, the energy of inspiration helps with the overall guidance sent to the world. That specific energy is known by different names, some call it the Holy Spirit, in other teachings it is known as the Holy Ghost. All inspiration is to help with the divine plan that directs individuals on Earth and those that follow the inspiration, transform their lives. Inspiration also ensures the divine plan stays on course." said the companion.

"Fascinating, absolutely fascinating," said Yusif, as he looked at the guards standing firm, as he made his way over to one of the bookshelves.

Yusif reached out to take a book from the shelf, however, his hand passed right through it. He tried again and his hand passed right through all the books on that section of the shelf.

That's strange, he thought to himself.

He noticed that the shelves around the room had signage above them, which showed how the books had been categorised, yet in this section, although the books were there and could be seen, their signage was blank. He looked across the room at another section, where there was clear information on the categories of the books, such as books about other worlds and galaxies and their inhabitants. This section fascinated Yusif. He walked over and plucked a book from the shelf, surprised he was able to pick up the book and not have his hand pass through it, as previously experienced, however, when he opened the book and flicked through its pages, they were all blank. Confused, drawing his eyebrows together, he looked over at his companions with a questioning gaze, raising his eyebrows, but they just smiled at him. He put the book back and pulled out another; it too contained blank pages. This puzzled Yusif because a few other beings pulled out a book from the same shelf, then sat down in a chair, reading its content.

"In the hereafter, curiosity is not a pursuit. You receive the book you need to help you grow and develop. If you have a task, then you will get a book that helps you complete that task. Other books in the library are there to help you prepare for work or heal yourself. That is why your hand passed through the books on that shelf and no words were on the pages of your next choice," the companion said to Yusif.

One of Yusif's companions beckoned him to another part of the library and told him to choose a book. He walked down the long line of books and noticed one of them had a faint green glow around it. Removing it from the shelf, he opened it and words appeared on the pages. Smiling, Yusif sat down to read.

As he read the book, the language and its expression were beautifully laid out. He was drawn right into the very words that he was reading. It was like he was surrounded in a bubble of energy as the background noise vanished. His awareness of the people in the room disappeared, as he was drawn into the words he was reading. The words activated his inner vision which enhanced his experience and understanding, rather than it being a purely intellectual exercise, he could visualise and feel the intention of the words he was reading. The words took him on a guided meditation, feeling as though he was living the words, causing him to dive deep within his soul, to a place he had not been before and he was surprised by what he found. It was strange, as images of his life played across his mind's eye, like a film reel in reverse, rapidly rewinding through time, as though someone had pressed fast-forward in reverse. The visions flickered and blurred at first but gained clarity as each frame of his life blended seamlessly together. He watched his older self gradually transform into a younger version as the picture wheel gradually slowed, coming to a full stop, leaving Yusif looking at himself, as a twelve-year-old boy, in his formative school years.

The book spoke to him about childhood traumas buried and forgotten but still remaining in the self. A memory relating to the words he was reading came into view. Although he saw it with his mind's eye, it seemed real, as if he were reliving the event in every detail again. As Yusif read and the vision played itself out, he watched it in full colour. He could even smell the essence and hear the words that other people were saying, as the vision endured. He saw a boy called Adam, who was in the year above him in school and who was responsible for bullying him. Although the bullying was mainly verbal and of a threatening nature, it caused Yusif to hold on to the fear as anger, as he was too small to understand or do anything about it. The emotional damage had created dark spots within his auric field, which manifested as blockages.

As the vision continued, it showed him other things about Adam that Yusif did not know or see at school. Adam was a large boy, becoming one of the tallest kids in the school as he aged and he used his size to throw his weight around in school, especially directed toward Yusif, during play time breaks and lunch periods. The vision turned to a time when Yusif had received one of Adam's threatening little talks, leaving Yusif feeling scared and intimidated, his own memory recalled that Adam had turned his back on him, giving Yusif the opportunity to scarper home as quickly as possible, however, the vision took a different direction from his memory and followed Adam to his home where Yusif discovered that Adam had also been the victim of bullying.

This part of the vision rewound back to an earlier time in Adam's life. Some of the teasing, cruel names and verbal bullying the younger Adam had been subjected to, by the bigger kids in the years above, had hurt him deeply, often resulting in him walking home from school in tears. His parents, especially his mother, had tried to console him, she even went into the school and spoke to the teachers about the matter. However, very little was done to prevent it continuing, in those early days. When the upset got too much for Adam, he would cry himself to sleep.

Now that Yusif had seen the other side of the story, his compassion for Adam found a place in his heart. This insight allowed Yusif to heal the pain that he carried around. He was able to forgive the bullying he suffered at school. After leaving school, Yusif had more-or-less forgotten about the bullying, however, in his later years, the memories had resurfaced as he reflected on his past. Although he tried to understand the reason, he could never come up with an answer as to why. Through his memory recall, the dark spots within his inner self, about the bullying he had gone through, had enlarged. This was all created through his negative emotional self, as he began to explore the incidents. Yusif did not realise how deeply the emotional pain had impacted him. He also became aware that if he had not read this book to help him understand his experiences, the emotional energy would have had to find another way of release. As with some experiences, to release the energy, there were three options. It must either play itself out as a reality, manifest as an illness in the body or be transformed, through healing, into light.

As he came to the end of the book, the images began to fade. He felt sorry for the pain Adam had to go through and he forgave the whole incident and expressed love in his heart. The love, trust and truth that flowed through Yusif, helped him transform the remaining dark spots in his aura into light.

It did not take hours to read the full book, as it might with traditional books, but Yusif knew he had come to the end of that particular story. The wisdom he gained from reading the book helped him to release and let go of past pain. As the vision dissolved, Yusif returned to sitting in the library, the sounds of those speaking and browsing the shelves returned and he was approached by the librarian, who had seen that he had finished the book and had come to return the book to its shelf. Her name was Khadija and she was known as 'The Mother of the Books'. She stood in front of him, her radiant aura causing Yusif to look up, feeling the humbleness emanating from her as she entered his presence. Khadija had come from the higher states of consciousness, to be of service and help those who wanted to learn. Yusif could also feel the wealth of information and in-depth knowledge she held, interwoven with a perception that Khadija was a very old soul. She had been around for eons, however, she still managed to retain her youthful appearance. She was filled with wisdom, knowledge and insights about every book in the library and could explain in depth, the wisdom behind the words contained within each book.

"Did you enjoy the book?" Khadija asked Yusif.

"Yes, very much so," he replied. "I believe I chose the correct book, it was perfect and allowed me to release that which was hidden from my view."

"That is the purpose of every book you see in this library. Energy works both ways. The question remains, did you choose the book or did the book choose you?" Khadija replied enigmatically.

This made Yusif smile as he pondered on what she had said, becoming enthralled in her presence. Khadija was wearing a green velvet robe that lightly brushed the floor as she moved and upon which pink dots of energy would appear, seemingly randomly. As Yusif spoke to her, he could feel himself falling deeper into what he could only describe as an ocean; an ocean of profound knowledge that Khadija held, along with a wisdom that permeated to the very depths of her being; he became lost for a moment.

"The information you read in here, will stay with you, to help you on your journey," said Khadija.

As they continued to speak about his experience with the book, Yusif noticed the gentle swaying movements that Khadija made as she was speaking to him. He watched as inspirational streams of energy flowed into her being. He knew it was through this energy that she spoke, almost hypnotically; it was the eloquent beauty of her words that drew him right into what she was saying, expressing the perfect order of the Heavens above. Each word in their right place.

"What about the books on the shelf where my hand passed right through?" Yusif enquired.

"Those books are waiting to be filled with new knowledge. God will reveal this information once the crystal appears on the tray at the top of this tower."

"Oh, that sounds like part of the quest my companions spoke about. Is what you speak of related to the quest connected to the island?" Yusif asked.

"Yes," replied Khadija.

"It seems a lot depends on that quest being completed," Yusif surmised, as he drifted off a little, to think about how important the quest was to the souls in Bakka.

"It will be completed when God is good and ready. Life is like an incomplete jigsaw puzzle. It is a captivating and immersive experience, that blends concentration, patience and the joy of revealing a complete picture from scattered fragments. All the pieces are there, jumbled up in the box, some are scattered on the table, others have already been put in place. As the pieces come together, through seeking clues that guide you to the piece's rightful placement, shape, edges and colours, the picture gradually builds and you begin to see the emerging structure, a glimpse of the hidden image, formulating the overall design. God is the master planner and architect, he moves people here and there, according to His will. As they fulfil their tasks, a small part of the plan becomes complete. God reveals elements of his plan to many people and as the master plan unfolds, souls who listen to the guidance that comes to them, complete their tasks according to the vision and instruction that they have been given. It is through their connection to the hereafter that they receive wisdom to help them on that journey. What they learn is shared with others and a gradual world transformation takes place. Every so often there is a nudge to keep the plan on course. Those who have raised their consciousness will understand that all things happen for a reason and if it is a part of God's plan, it will manifest." Said Khadija, demonstrating that depth of knowledge and wisdom Yusif had felt.

Yusif smiled and nodded in deference to Khadija, noticing, as he looked down, that she was wearing a black pair of slippers that seemed incongruous with the rest of her attire, raising an eyebrow. Khadija noticed his expression and smiled reverently.

"I wear these slippers as a symbolic gesture, to remind me that I still have much to learn and many miles to travel," Khadija explained.

As Khadija said these words, she slowly tilted her head backwards and rotated it in a small circle as she slowly closed and opened her eyes, as if she was blinking in slow motion. She was bathing in the beautiful love that flowed from the Heavens above and Yusif was himself humbled by the gesture, her movement and the sincerity of her expression.

"Well, it has truly been an honour coming to this library and meeting you, Khadija. This world and the love and wisdom it has to offer, has opened up a whole new understanding to me," said Yusif, as he glimpsed his companions heading for the exit. "Thank you, Khadija, the time here and the revelations, have given me a great insight, which will surely help me in my understanding of myself. All that this world has to offer will remain and help me on this journey," said Yusif.

"You will be welcome here anytime… hurry now, your companions are about to leave," said Khadija.

Yusif excused himself from her presence and got up from his chair. He caught up with his companions and they told him they were going up to the next level.

TRAVELLING THROUGH TIME

Once again, Yusif and his companions made their way along corridors to a room from which they would be able to travel to the top section of the structure. Yusif felt a different kind of energy in that room, it had a noticeable essence to it, that was different from the energy that allowed him to travel up and down, to and from, the different levels. At the far side of the room, he could see white light energy flowing up towards the ceiling, which looked like tiny rain drops but they were rising instead of falling.

"Feel the energy in this room, attune yourself to it," instructed one of the companions.

They all walked over to the far side of the room and stepped into the light energy. As they did, they started to ascend up through a hole in the ceiling, up to the top section of the crystal structure where they came to a stop.

"Stay in the energy for a little longer," said another companion.

Yusif closed his eyes and bathed in the energy, while the companions stepped out. After a few seconds, a couple of beings appeared next to them. One of them was his friend Paul, the other was Sara, who Yusif had met earlier when they had travelled to the planet Zamzam. Both were well-journeyed souls. They frequently came here to use the teleports to transport themselves to other worlds, where they would work with the angelic forces.

"Before you step out of this rising energy, we needed to adjust your vibration to a different frequency," explained Paul.

He passed Yusif a crystal orb and asked him to hold it. Sara stepped forward and put her hands on the crystal and the energy around Yusif changed colour. The droplets were now light green in colour.

Once the adjustments were made, Yusif stepped out of the energy, joined his friends and the companions and they all moved to another room. They explained to Yusif that only highly-evolved and highly-skilled beings could use the teleportation portal, which was housed in this top part of the crystal structure, through which they could enter Bakka on their way to other worlds in and around the solar system.

Yusif noticed that the vibrational energy in this section of the crystal structure had a coolness about it. It was not like the cold you experience when outside in the wind, rain or snow, it was, strangely, a coolness without the chill factor. Within this new energy, there was yet another stream of energy. It seemed to be made up of a complex and ever-changing digitised stream of symbols and numbers, when viewed in the periphery of his vision, it was pink in colour. It felt very modern and futuristic, compared to the other marvels he had witnessed, like it was calculating endlessly and had a precise exactitude to its flow. It was brought to Yusif's attention that this energy from the crystals enabled these inter-dimensional travellers to pinpoint with accuracy their destination and time of arrival, as they travelled to places afar.

"This energy calculates the days and the nights, the hours and the seconds. Even on Earth, the rising and the setting of the sun, the waxing and the waning of the moon are controlled and calculated by a similar energy." Paul explained. "God is the creator of all energy. Through this particular energy, the precision of whole galaxies are kept in order. Each planet, star and galaxy are swimming along its path with perfect precision and order. God created crystals as a medium through which certain kinds of energy can be channelled. With humanity unable to control their thought processes, He created all these different kinds of crystals to help balance and realign many unbalanced energies. This understanding can be likened to the way God uses light as a vehicle, that He might guide us out of the darkness." Paul disclosed.

There were a number of guarded shimmering doors in the room that contained many crystals and crystal orbs. The guards ensured nothing unexpected or prohibited came through the teleportation crystals.

"The beings who use the transporter crystals receive their workload via their guides. Their guides live and work in even higher vibrational states of consciousness, their role is to oversee inter-dimensional travel from Bakka and their consciousness encircles entire galaxies; they command sight of all things within their awareness," explained the companions.

"How old are some of these souls who watch over whole galaxies?" Asked Yusif.

"It is impossible to say. A yearly cycle on one world can be two years in another world. In some worlds, time is not important. Different worlds have different concepts of time. The soul lives and will continue living after its life on Earth. There is but the beginning and the ending of something. What happens in between depends on the soul. Some beings in Bakka travel to far distant places, where they work to help with their evolution. They respond only to the will of the greater good. They work behind the scenes, in the vibrations beyond the realities of the worlds they visit. Some souls can spend many years in these places, helping and working with those who are ready to be elevated. However, in the hereafter, it is but a blink of an eye," explained Paul.

"In some realities, just like on Earth, souls can become lost to the illusion. Volunteers step forward to be of service, delivering inspiration and guidance, as they watch over certain souls. Both learn from the other. As the soul in the physical reality meditates, they begin to recognise true wisdom and become more aware that through listening and being in service to others, they expand and grow. Their inner light shines and ensures that the path to God and the higher dimensions, remains open. Through the light and the doing of good deeds, God's plan continues to flourish," Sara continued.

"Inspiration has come to me via my angels. They have informed me that there are some tasks they would like us to complete, for which you are to accompany us. Your companions will stay behind on this occasion and you, Yusif, will travel with Sara and I on this trip," said Paul.

Those in the hereafter never miss an opportunity to give guidance or offer help to others, Yusif thought to himself.

Yusif's companions let him know they would be aware of his return after the completion of the task.

"We will continue our journey to the island, on your return," said one of the companions.

Sara walked over to one of the teleporter crystals, followed by Paul and Yusif. As they got closer to the teleporter crystal, Yusif was feeling unsure about what to expect.

"Create a protective light around yourself, like you did when we visited Zamzam, to stop your energy from being drained. It will also repel any negative thought activity sent out by those who are struggling to cope, as we complete our tasks," Sara instructed Yusif. "When you focus on a crystal, the place we are to visit will appear. A light will manifest and surround us, and then we will be carried in an arc of light, to the destination in the crystal. Once we have completed the work required of us, a light will appear that will bring us back here. Sometimes it may appear and take us somewhere else before our final return to this room. In the end though, we will be brought back to this room," said Sara.

She paused for a moment, while Yusif readied himself for the journey.

"When you are ready, look into the crystal Yusif," said Sara.

Yusif stepped forward and they all looked into the crystal. The crystal immediately began to clear and a picture of Earth came into view. An energy arc of light force radiated out from the crystal until it surrounded Paul, Sara and Yusif and they suddenly found themselves travelling at great speed down a tunnel of beautiful lights. There were two sudden thrusts forward, in which Yusif felt himself being carried part of the way, by a being that he did not recognise. When they eventually came to a stop, they found themselves just beyond where Earth becomes clothed in physical matter.

Sara explained that they were there in their spiritual forms and could not be seen by the majority of people in the physical world, only by other spiritual beings.

Yusif recognised the place straight away, as the city of Bradford where he lived. He looked around to get his exact bearings and then followed Paul and Sara along the street. Yusif found it strange that in his spiritual form he could smell the aroma of the city, just as in Bakka. He was also intrigued, as he watched other spiritual beings as they worked and oversaw those on Earth. The other spiritual beings were not dressed in any particular way and some of the helpers were actually those who had lived on Earth before. They did not all present themselves as angels with wings. They would come to the person offering them guidance in an appearance that would be recognised by the person on Earth. They would deliver their messages of inspiration to the soul over whom they were guardians. Yusif carried a facial expression of amazement, as he watched how they laboured, the toil that went on behind the scenes, to inspire someone or bring people together. This bringing together, or 'karma', as most people know it, was connected to the 'Spiritual Law of Cause and Effect'. Souls are brought together to work out some of their past mistakes. Yusif also noticed that some guides and angels would keep a distance from some souls under their care, while others were quite close up and this puzzled him.

"Those spiritual beings that keep a distance, do so because of the thought expressions of the soul walking around in a physical body. Earth is a place where souls of varying degrees of conscious awareness come together to learn. Their expression directly conveys their inner spiritual condition, which either attracts or repels their guardian angels and guides. Angels and guides are attracted by love, which creates a beautiful smell, like that of flowers or perfumes, whereas ego, hatred, backbiting and gossip, creates a foul smell, so their guardian angels and guides will step back, waiting for that one moment where the soul emanates even just a small amount of love, after which, the guardian or guide can send to the tortured soul inspiration in a bid that they might listen and choose to begin the healing process," Sara explained, once again seeming to read Yusif's mind.

They moved quickly through the Earth plane, part walking, part floating and the physical world passed by quickly as they travelled. As they slowed down and came to a stop, Paul and Sara pointed to the vehicle of Yusif's neighbour, Ali, sitting in an endless line of traffic on the motorway. Yusif realised that they had indeed become stuck in traffic, just as Alisha had told him on the phone earlier that day (although it seemed like days or weeks ago since Yusif had taken that call, as he felt he had been in Bakka for much longer than he had). Alisha, Ali's wife, was fumbling around with her mobile phone, the one she had called Yusif on, still trying to get it to work. As they sat in the car waiting for the traffic to move forward, their children, Areeba and Subhan, had fallen asleep in the back seats. Alisha pulled the back cover of the phone off the phone and took out the battery. She rubbed it in her hands, hoping that it would become re-energised. She then put the phone back together, silently wishing that the phone would come back to life, so that she could try contacting Yusif again, to finish the conversation they had started.

"We have been stuck in this traffic jam for quite a while, we cannot have moved more than a mile in the last two hours." said Alisha, as she pushed the buttons on the phone, trying to get it to work.

This made Yusif realise how different the concept of time was in the hereafter. He had seen and done much more than he could have fit into the same period of time on Earth.

"We are not going to be home in time," said Alisha, as she looked at her watch, then checked it against the clock in the car. "What are we going to do?" She worried, as she looked at her sleeping children in the back of the car. "Is there another way we can go? What time do you think we will get home? Can we stop at the super store to get some food on the way home? What has happened and why is it taking so long?"

"We will get there when we get there. You should have charged the phone before we left," said Ali, not too happy about the number of questions his wife was bombarding him with, as if there was anything he could do to remedy the situation they were in.

Yusif was just about to ask Paul and Sara if they knew what the message was, when Paul said:

"Let's go."

They took Yusif to the front of the traffic jam that had blocked the motorway, where he saw that there had been a serious accident. A couple had been removed from a vehicle and were laying on hospital trollies by the roadside. Both of them had serious external and internal injuries. Yusif could see that the couple were actually now in the spirit world, as their spiritual bodies were standing on the grass verge, near to where their physical bodies laid, watching, as the ambulance services tried one last time to resuscitate them. Unable to do any more for the physical bodies, the ambulance crew pronounced them both as deceased.

The couple looked over in the direction of Paul, Sara and Yusif and were about to ask them who they were and why they were there, when other spirit forms started to appear to them. These were of friends and family members who had already passed over. Yusif watched as they reached out to the couple, who on recognising their beloved friends and family, welcomed them with greetings and hugs. They all ascended to Heaven, leaving the physical world and their physical bodies behind.

Once the souls of the couple had left, Paul and Sara then took Yusif to a part of the city he knew well and as they walked down the street, Yusif saw a few people with whom he had previously had conversations with, at some time or another and Yusif smiled at the recollection. They continued their journey and made their way to a part of the city that was known for criminal activity, where petty criminals would hang out on street corners with each other. Among those people, Yusif recognised his old school acquaintance, Adam, the boy who had bullied him at school. He could see that Adam was still a troubled young man, who had failed to overcome his own bullying incidents from the boys in the years above him, which were still impacting on his life, even now. He had obviously found it difficult to move on from the anger of his past. Paul explained that Adam's state of mind had grown worse over the years and he had not helped himself by continuing to throw his own weight around. Furthermore, it was the death of Adam's mother that had really added to his inner rage. He was now holding on to a lot of guilt and with his state of mind being what it was, Adam was finding it hard to make good decisions. He had not been the best of sons while his mother was alive; he did not listen to her and thought he knew best. His mother could see beyond the choices and friends he was making after he left school and she had tried her best to warn him about some of the company he was keeping. The people he was involved with were older than him and he was still being bullied, as he tried to make his way up through the ranks of the criminal element, his ultimate plan being to make fast money and then move on.

His mother had explained to him that there were no ways to get rich quick, but as usual, he did not listen to her. She had also known that he was getting too deeply involved with those people and things would not end well for him as a result. One of the reasons why he carried so much guilt was that while he was out partying, his mother had suffered a massive stroke and had been taken into hospital. With additional complications, it was there that she had passed away and was gone from his life (or so he thought). His last conversation with his mother had been an argument, after which he had disappeared for a week, to indulge in his passions and criminal behaviours. It had been during that time that his mother had died and he was completely unaware of the fact. The argument and the fact that he was not there for her in her final days, kept surfacing in his mind. He knew she was right in what she said but he was too foolish to acknowledge this truth.

Yusif could see Adam's mother and grandmother as spiritual beings standing beside him, trying to inspire him to do what was right. They were desperate to pass on a message that she was fine and with his grandmother in Heaven; that he should not carry so much guilt around with him.

Paul, Sara and Yusif approached Adam's mother and Sara explained that when Yusif returned to the physical world, he would pass on the message to Adam that they still existed on a higher plane and were doing well. So that Adam would know Yusif was telling the truth, he would also reveal facts and situations, that only Adam could know about his mother and grandmother, as verification. After Sara and Yusif had finished speaking with the mother and grandmother, their guardian angels appeared and they both ascended back to the Heaven they had descended from.

"It is their continued love for Adam that united them and although he was not the best of sons, his parents and family members, who have passed away, still love him. They have access to the bigger picture of life itself and now know why Adam is the way he is throughout his time on Earth. They know why he was born into the world through them and of the lessons they all had to learn from their life in the world. They were his Earthly parents, but each soul has its own journey and is accountable for their own choices and deeds. The only way the parents could learn their lessons, was to have an unruly son. His mother had to learn to let go of her children and he had to learn to make better choices. These lessons were very simple and at the same time very important to learn." Sara told Yusif.

"Adam's guilt has created a wall of anguish that surrounds him. He finds it hard to acknowledge the inspiration sent to free him and even though Adam heard the inspiration, he has chosen not to follow it. The inspiration has become like a cloud that passed by. He believes that following a path of feelings and love, is a weak way to live if you want to get on in life. He has chosen to ignore the truth that was sent to help him. Unfortunately, through the 'Law of Attraction', he has attracted souls worse than himself. He cannot see that they are using him for their own ends. Due to him listening and following such lower vibrating thoughts, certain events are in the process of manifesting." Paul continued.

"Do not go looking for Adam, you will be guided to meet him soon after returning to Earth. Most of his hard lessons are now behind him and he has done some serious soul searching for answers, leading him to accept responsibility for much that has taken place in his life, so, when you meet him, he should be more receptive and hopefully friendlier towards you," said Sara.

Certain thoughts and feeling started to rise up within Yusif, as he reflected on the bullying he endured during his school years. This is when the information from the book he had read in the library on Bakka, seemed to rise up within him, to counterbalance any ill feelings that might try to surface. Yusif closed his eyes for a moment, to remember the words in the book and reach out to hold on to the truth.

"I am sorry for the bullying you suffered at the hands of Adam," said Adam's mother.

Yusif opened his eyes, Adam's mother had returned with her guardian angel, her kind voice dispersing any ill feelings.

"It's fine, there is always a reason for everything that happens. We have to look within to find it. Sometimes it is beyond our vision of the present moment and it may not be seen immediately but working through it, will reveal it and all will be fine," replied Yusif.

"We can see with Adam that there is a window of opportunity coming up in his life. He was trying to work things out within himself, but he kept slipping back to his old ways. Previous associates will temp him into doing something from which he will lose hope of redemption. Adam will still have the freedom of choice but the information Yusif is to relay to Adam will help him balance that choice. We are hopeful things will start to get better for him, if he accepts the opportunity," said Sara.

"Each soul needs to approach their own soul, as to why things happen in their life. In their acceptance of responsibility, they increase their chance of saving themselves. Self-restraint from dark thoughts shows the soul's true striving in the cause of God," explained Paul.

Yusif was amazed how Paul and Sara could continue an explanation, from where the other left off, it was like they each knew what the other one was thinking. Even more interesting, was the fact that they each knew when the other had stopped. It was perfect synchronicity.

"Those in the hereafter do indeed come and help those on Earth. Inspiration and wisdom are sent to every soul. It gives balance to the soul and creates choice. Because God granted humankind the freewill to choose, we in the hereafter cannot interfere with their final decision. We can only inspire them now and again. Every soul receives this guidance, through their evolved self. The asking for help opens the door to receiving that guidance. Those that listen, in their choices, can learn to elevate their consciousness or they can fall into ruin," added Sara.

As Paul and Sara continued to talk, Yusif began to clearly see and understand how each soul attracts to itself, reaping what it has sown. According to their degree of acceptance or rejection, they start to build a sustainable foundation of thought on which they stand.

"By understanding and learning to express unconditional love towards all, you become more. Those who meditate, learn new wisdom as they reach out with their consciousness, hear the wisdom that leads them to truth and right actions. This wisdom comes from the stations above them. They begin to understand how the 'Spiritual Laws' and the light, both play a part in their life. Hold on to spiritual wisdom. It does not matter from which religion you gain your wisdom, seek where you can, for the truth. You will know spiritual wisdom when you hear it as real words of wisdom speak to your heart," said Paul.

"Thank you, your words of wisdom and insight are a real inspiration that keep my feet firmly planted in the truth," said Yusif, to Paul and Sara.

We left Adam and the group he was with and headed to our next location. In our spiritual forms, we were able to move through the Earthly plane so fast, we could break every human athletic or speed records. We floated along on a river of energy, travelling the streets of Bradford, eventually coming to a stop, where we witnessed a couple who were walking precariously. Yusif could tell that they were not focusing on other people around them, as they pushed their way passed them. It was as though they were trying not to bump into people purposely, but they did not care if they did. Many people had to swerve or turn aside to avoid a collision. The woman, in her late forties, had her arm locked around the arm of her husband, her face pointing downwards at the ground, as she tried to hide her tears of emotional upset. From the hereafter, Paul, Sara and Yusif could see dark energy swirling around the couple due to their state of mind. Yusif could not help himself; he looked a little deeper into what was making the man and woman's energy expression so dark.

As Yusif delved into their situation, he saw a young woman in her thirties, coming out of a clothing store, with several shopping bags hooked over her arms. Her long hair had blown to one side and it hung down over the side of her face, obscuring her view of the oncoming car. She was looking down at her phone as she stepped off the curb and into the road. The driver was unable to stop in time. The young woman was thrown into the air by the car and as she came back down, she hit her head hard as she landed on the tarmacked road. The screeching of the tyres on the road, followed by the screams of onlookers witnessing the accident, caused others to stop in their tracks and turn around to see what was causing the outburst. The vehicle came to a halt and the male driver jumped out and ran over to the woman lying on the road, just as a few others rushed over to see what help they could offer. One man, on the phone to his wife, quickly ended the call and dialled the emergency services. Yusif could tell from the image that the woman had sustained a serious injury. It didn't take long for the ambulance to arrive at the scene, where paramedics rushed to the woman's side to assess her injuries and administer immediate stabilising care for her, putting her on a backboard, applying a neck brace and applying pressure to the obvious head trauma, which was bleeding profusely. Yes, it was a serious accident indeed! The paramedics lifted the young woman on to a trolley, loaded it into the ambulance and rushed her to the emergency room at the local hospital.

Through reading the couple in this way, Yusif realised that in the hereafter, for every kind of query regarding knowledge or an experience one has in relation to what one is seeing, information is miraculously made available; that each soul is like an open book. Nothing is hidden from those who have eyes to see. Knowledge was granted to Yusif about the young woman injured in the accident, which turned out to be the daughter of the couple walking down the street. The husband and wife had received a phone call from the police, informing them that their daughter had been in an accident and she was now in the hospital; that they should get there as quickly as possible, where they would be given more information.

The young woman's parents were distraught and thinking only of reaching the hospital as quickly as possible and this was why they were so upset and preoccupied, that they did not take notice of how they were walking, who they were bumping into and moreover, didn't care about anything else at that time. Luckily, the young woman had enough identification on her so her parents could be contacted and immediately after the police had spoken to them, they received another call from the hospital. The attending registrar told the parents that their daughter had sustained a serious head injury and some other, not as severe, physical injuries from landing on the ground. The doctors needed permission from the parents to put her into a medically induced coma to reduce the blood flow to her brain, which would help any swelling to go down in order to stabilise her condition.

As Sara, Paul and Yusif continued walking a little further down the street, a female came rushing towards them, catching Yusif by surprise. He was not able to move out of her way in time, so he closed his eyes and braced himself for a collision, expecting to feel the impact and hear the thud it would make as it happened, however, what did happen brought Yusif to a sudden full stop and moment of relief. The woman ran straight through him. It was such a strange feeling. He immediately knew she was not like the other people walking around in the physical world. As she passed through Yusif, there was something about the texture and quality of her auric energy that surprised him. He had the strangest feeling that this woman was aware he was there and that she had made a connection with him in the hereafter. Although she could not see him, she stopped and turned around with a smile on her face. By this time Yusif had opened his eyes and he could see that she was smiling and filling with light, which radiated a beautiful, loving energy.

"Hello, what can I do for you?" She said, telepathically.

Paul stepped forward and spoke to her. "What is your name?" he asked.

"Tasneem," she replied.

Paul moved closer to her to help with the communication. "We are on a mission of mercy from God. We have a small task for you, Tasneem, " said Paul.

"How can I serve?" she asked, as she pulled her coat around herself.

Paul explained that in a few minutes a couple were going to pass by and he projected an image of the couple into Tasneem's mind.

"Could you kindly pass on a message, to help a couple in need?" Paul asked.

"Gladly, you know I love to work for God and the spiritual world." Tasneem replied.

"Their daughter is in hospital after being hit by a vehicle. Do not worry, Nazish will make a full recovery and we would like you to reassure her parents, the couple I mentioned, of this."

A few minutes later, the couple came walking briskly down the other side of the street. Tasneem had to run, to try and catch up with them.

"Call out their daughter's name, Nazish," Paul transmitted to Tasneem.

"NAZISH!" shouted Tasneem, from across the street.

This immediately caught the attention of the man's wife. She stopped and pulled back on her husband's arm. Tasneem caught up with them and passed on the message as requested. An image of a watch and a bouquet of flowers, popped into Tasneem's mind and she used this to ensure the couple knew she was talking about their daughter. She told them that the special watch was a gift to the father and reminded the mother of the flowers that their daughter used to bring home for her. With this validation, they relaxed and calmed down, although, they were looking at Tasneem beseechingly, as though she might have more information.

Tasneem looked upward and to the right, as though she was pondering some conundrum, however, in reality, she was receiving further inspiration about the reasoning behind Nazish's accident. Tasneem, looked back toward the parents and started to explain why the accident had happened and that, really, it couldn't be classified as an accident, because it was Nazish's wish to experience this happening, in order for her to reach a higher spiritual experience. "You see, the accident had led to her being sedated and put into a medically induced coma, which was her chosen pathway of enlightenment. Through this accident, as she lays in a coma, she will have an out of body experience. She will be permitted to remember all the details of the event as she comes out of her body." Tasneem told them. This was the information we passed on to Tasneem, so that we might complete our task.

"Do not to be too upset by the physical condition of your daughter when you see her. She will not be in any pain. By the time she leaves hospital, her internal injuries will be minimal. Her bodily wounds will heal and the bruising will disappear. When she comes out of her coma, you need to listen to what she says about the experience. The direction of her life is about to change. Once she recovers, she will write books about her experience that will bring comfort to many people. These books will give hope and bring a reassurance that the hereafter, is a real place and not a myth or fairy tale. Remember, there are no mistakes. Trust in God and have faith," Tasneem said to Nazish's parents.

Once they had listened to what Tasneem had to say, the darkness around the couple started to fade, as their minds calmed down from over thinking. A few more tears were shed from the mother, but they were from a different place, they were happier tears. The couple thanked Tasneem for the understanding and guidance she had passed on to them. After the couple had left, Paul also thanked Tasneem for passing on the message.

"It was a pleasure to be of service," said Tasneem, as she stood there smiling, the people passing in the street having no idea what had taken place.

Sara moved close to Tasneem and whispered in her ear. "Mariyah is coming. It is wished that you help her."

Tasneem understood this message, as it was something she had heard before. She had taught a number of people how to open their awareness to the world of the hereafter.

"I will be waiting and looking forward to meeting her," said Tasneem, as she looked at her phone to see what time it was.

Before Tasneem left, Yusif saw something of Tasneem's future. Tasneem was thinking that she would now be late for work, because she would miss her train at the station she was originally heading to, however, what was interesting, was the difference in perception, additional knowledge provided. The connection with Tasneem had revealed to Yusif a greater insight. There is an ordered sequence of events known by many as synchronicity. It was revealed to Yusif that because Tasneem had missed her train, while she was waiting for the next train, she would in fact meet her future husband, get married and be blessed with two lovely children. This again clarified to Yusif that there was a divine plan at work; that there are no mistakes. It also revealed how little we know about what is really going on in our lives; that there is always a bigger picture to consider.

THE WAITRESS AND THE ANGELS

After leaving Tasneem, they journeyed on, to a quiet part of the city centre, where they visited a café. The door through which they entered the café, was down a narrow alley and as they moved along the small passageway leading into the main part of the café, Yusif felt a very weird sensation throughout his body. His arms and legs had suddenly become leaden and more effort was required to be able to take a step. In fact, so noticeable was the change, that they all staggered for a few steps while they tried to compensate for the extra weight. *Strange*, thought Yusif, *am I becoming physical again? Why? What is happening?* They walked through the café towards a table and sat down, but Yusif was puzzled as the other people in the café seemed to be able to see them, their eyes following them as they moved through the café. It would appear that those in the physical world could now see them.

"What is happening?" Yusif asked, as he leaned forward and whispered to Paul and Sara.

"God has power over all things and He always has a plan. Act normal, let's see how this plays out," said Paul.

"Has this ever happened to you before Sara?" Asked Yusif.

"No, it's been a long time since I have felt the weight of a physical body, let alone able to see myself as I once was," she said, as she looked at her reflection in the window.

Paul and Yusif mirrored Sara's action by looking at their reflections in the windowpane. They watched as Sara adjusted her hair. She tried out several options, half pony tail, length over the shoulder, all cascading down her back and simply fluffing it up with her hands, moving her head from side to side and giving it a shake, as she settled on leaving it resting over one shoulder. Paul and Yusif watched her admiringly, as she tended to herself, both equally aware of her inner and outer beauty. Paul and Yusif put their hands to their chins and nodded in approval at their own unexpected youthful appearance, as they also checked their hair, turning their heads from side to side. Yusif was surprised to realise that they all had younger appearances, looking no more than twenty-two years of age. They all then turned back around in their seats, to face each other once again at the table.

"Souls do not age in the spiritual world. Their appearance is according to their own self-image," said Sara.

"Imagine if my physical body walked in now," mused Yusif, as he pondered on what they were going to do next, in a café, without money for food or drinks.

This seemed to amuse Paul and Sara, as they smiled at one another and let out a little chuckle of laughter. Although Yusif, Paul and Sara had denser physical bodies, they retained their spiritual awareness and could still see the things of the hereafter. They could also see the very corporeal waitress coming in their direction, to take their order. Paul put his hands together and made a small supplication to God for some money. When he opened his hands, they were all amazed to see there was about five-hundred pounds in his hands, crispy twenty-pound notes, all stacked neatly.

"Are you planning on buying the place?" Yusif asked, with a cheeky smile on his face.

This again amused Paul and Sara and they all laughed. A few other people in the café turned their heads in their direction, to see what the laughter was about.

The waitress, called Joanne, arrived at their table to take their order and it was not long before she came back with their food and drinks. Paul handed all the cash to Joanne and she quickly protested that it was way too much and tried to hand the majority of it back to Paul, however, he refused to take it. She looked puzzled and shocked as she looked back at him, quickly looking at Sara and Yusif, as if she expected them to tell Paul he was making a mistake, but they remained silent but smiled at Joanne.

"What is happening?" Joanne asked, her face a picture of confusion.

"Please, pay for our food and keep the rest of the money for yourself," said Paul, politely smiling and giving a nod of his head.

Sara and Yusif also nodded their approval and smiled at the waitress.

"You deserve it," said Sara, as she flicked her hair back with her hand.

The waitress smiled, but still had a cast in her eyes that said she couldn't quite believe what was happening. "Are you sure?" she asked, trying to make it clear that she was completely surprised by the gesture. "Why? This is too much! Oh my God, I can't believe it?" she continued, as she quickly counted the money in her hand.

"I can't believe this," she said. "This is exactly the amount I need. I was so afraid that I would be unable to pay my rent and bills this month. Last week, my daughter was ill and I was unable to work. I cannot thank you enough. You really are an angel," said Joanne, as she put most of the money into her apron pocket. She walked over to the till and paid for the food they had ordered.

This made Yusif laugh out loud followed by apologies to the other customers for interrupting their tranquillity.

Joanne went back to her station and continued to serve other customers who came into the café. The customers sat either in conversation with their friends or colleagues or just relaxing, looking out of the window, watching as people went about their daily lives.

Yusif watched the other customers and could see their thoughts, wishes and dreams emanating from their bodies, in the form of orbs of energy filled with pictures, popping out and hovering above their heads. The energy contained both light and colour and was beautiful to look at. Most of the people he watched had beautiful auras, filled with loving energy and Yusif was fascinated by the way those auras interacted and affected other people, as they came closer together.

He turned to look out the window. He could see those outside, their light would extend outwards to surround people as they passed by, with some of the light being absorbed by those it touched. Yusif could see their energy field change as they received the light energy and he could sense that the person felt a little better after receiving it. Yusif watched as a couple hugged each other in welcome, as though they had not seen each other for a while and it was so nice to see the exchange of love, energy and light around them. The loving energy radiated far and wide, affecting everything it touched.

There were also some people whose thoughts manifested like puffs of smoke, quickly fading away to nothing and some whose thoughts fired away in all directions, just like arrows being fired in a multitude of directions. Yusif was saddened, as he observed the majority of those thoughts being returned to their senders, as no one claimed or absorbed them and Yusif knew that they were caused by the negative emotions those people were feeling about the direction in which their lives were going. There were so many different variations of light and darkness swirling around the different people as they walked up and down the street. Yusif could see that there was a great feeling of loneliness and despair surrounding some people but he could also see that it was their own choice, to cut themselves off from the divine guidance that came to them. Their current self-expression and choices came down to a point in their youthful lives, where they decided to believe or not to believe.

"Every cry for help is heard," said Paul. "An answer is sent to the soul via their guardian angel and those who pay attention will become aware of the answer. Even if they are not paying attention or have not opened themselves up to receive those answers, God will use other methods to try and reach those souls, so the answer can come in a variety of ways. The most direct way is sent into the mind and we call this inspiration which can come as feeling, words or symbols. Every possible way to help humankind is sent to every soul. The recognition of signs and symbols can make such a difference in their life if they pay attention. They can lead to roads filled with many more possibilities in their life. In their choices, we can see if they are ready to be open, to accept divine guidance from ourselves. Into their mind will flow the wisdom to help them understand what they are seeing. This recognition within them is a beautiful gift, given to them by God. When they return to us, they will see all the hard work that went on behind the scenes. Other ways are through physical signs and symbols that can be seen in the Earthly plane, by those who missed the inner messages. It may come to them as an image that jogs their memory about something, or they may see a written word or number that reminds you about a special time or place. As with all things spiritual, they have to want to see the signs and symbols, then they will recognise them," Paul continued.

"Thank you, Paul, even in Bakka, your words of wisdom were of great value," said Yusif.

A guardian angel appeared next to Sara, Paul and Yusif.

"I too, was listening while you were speaking. What honourable words you speak," said the divine being of light, who then faded away and disappeared.

"We are aware that people in the world are told to pray, however, the majority are not taught how to listen or see the answer. Once they learn how to listen and see the answer, they will be amazed at how their life changes. They will become aware that they have always been guided. The thoughts they think and the actions that follow, will be done with the greatest intention of love. Life is about looking and learning. If you have never looked, you will never learn," said Paul.

They all nodded in acknowledgement and approval.

Some of the people who were sat in the café looked over in the direction of the three of them and watched as they nodded to one another. It was not too long before relatives of some of the café's patrons, family who had previously passed over into the spiritual world, began to materialise, as they wanted us to pass on messages to their family members in the physical world. They wanted to do this to ease the lives of the ones that they had left behind. As they looked at the people sat in the café, Sara, Paul and Yusif could see that no one was suffering to such an extent that they were contemplating taking their own lives and Sara explained to the visiting relatives, that her small group were not here for those sitting at tables in the café, so they shouldn't be worried about that. She told them that they were actually on a special mission of mercy, for another person and that they should return to the Heavens from where they came. Some of them did protest a little but apologised and left. Paul, Sara and Yusif, had other people to see and would not be sidetracked by every statement of concern or request for help.

"What other hidden delights does the hereafter have to offer?" Yusif queried.

"There is so much that is hidden from humanity. Even we say, 'Allah knows best, He knows all things'," said Sara.

When they had finished their snack, they piled their plates up on the table, for collection when Paul said, "I have received inspiration about another task we have yet to complete. Wait here Yusif, we need to speak to the other waitress sat at a small table by the side of the counter."

Paul and Sara got up from the table and made their way over to where the second waitress was sitting, tucked away in a small space, partly hidden by the side of the counter, taking her own lunch break. She had watched Sara, Paul and Yusif come into the café and seen them order their food from Joanne, so as they approached her, she stood up and took a step forward. As they conversed, Yusif saw a couple of beautiful spirit beings appear next to the young woman; her guardian angels. They had drawn close and were awaiting their turn to speak with her, but the young woman had felt their presence and became a little hesitant and filled with a mixture of emotions that she drew back from Paul and Sara. Sara reached out and held the young woman's hand.

"Do not be afraid. We are from the hereafter; we are on a mission of mercy and you are on our list of people to speak to in this world. We are sent by God and have a duty to help a number of people."

The young woman pulled back a little more, releasing her hand from Sara's. She wanted to believe, but the world had taught her not to trust and, in its place, there had manifested thoughts of caution and self-doubt.

"You know your guardian angels are here with us," explained Sara, as she looked straight at the young woman.

She could not deny having felt something a few moments ago, a presence that was somewhat familiar and she narrowed her eyes into a squint as she looked back at Sara, trying to analyse her and determine whether she could possibly be speaking the truth to her.

"Your guardian angels want to step forward. They want to show themselves to you and start working with you," said Sara.

This was the last thing the young woman expected to hear coming from Sara and it made her mind race back to the time, she herself, had heard a voice in her head, speaking more clearly than the people around her. From squinting eyes, she now opened her eyes wide and gave them both a stare as if to say, "what did you say to me?"

How do they know about guardian angels? The young woman thought to herself.

"We know they are here waiting to speak to you," said Paul.

"What?" Said the young woman. *Wait a minute, did I say that out loud or did I say that in my head? How do they know what I was thinking?* She asked herself.

The fact that Paul answered the questions that she was thinking, took her by surprise.

"They are right here, right now?" The Young woman responded.

"Yes, right here, right now," confirmed Sara.

Sara reached out for her hand again. The young woman smiled and placed her hand back in Sara's.

"We are here to offer you some help and advice. What is your name?"

"Mariyah," replied the young woman.

"Mariyah, we are tasked with helping those who are ready to awaken. Let me help you to see a little more clearly," said Sara.

As the energy from Sara encircled Mariyah, she saw her guardian angels in full, for the first time. Mariyah's mouth dropped open when her guardian angel came into view. She stepped back, this time in amazement. Mariyah looked back and forth a few times, first at Paul and Sara, then to her guardian angels, fearing to believe what she was seeing. To the rest of the people in the café, they only saw Mariyah moving her head from side to side, as she switched between Paul, Sara and her guardian angels. No one else in the café, except Yusif, was able to see Mariyah's guardian angels. Paul and Sara continued talking to Mariyah, explaining she had some special work to do for God.

It was indeed a 'red pill' or a 'blue pill' moment for Mariyah. Yusif turned his gaze and looked out of the window. Outside, a family of four, two adults, a daughter of about eight years of age and their small son of around five years old, were walking past the café window and as they passed the café, the young boy looked through the window and pointed. The child could see Paul, Sara, Mariyah and the guardian angels, standing in a group and he pulled on his mother's hand and pointed towards Mariyah, causing the rest of the family to stop and look through the café window, to see what he was pointing at. The mother looked down at her young child.

"We do not have time to stop, you can have something to eat once we get to your aunties house," she told her son.

"Look mummy, look, over there," he said, with a beaming smile on his face.

He pulled his hand free of his mother, ran up to the window and pressed his little hands and face up against it. Yusif could see the little boy wriggling and bobbing up and down as he gazed through the window. The mother looked through the café window again and only saw people sitting at tables and a couple of people chatting to a waitress. She did not see what the young child saw. The small boy looked up at Yusif and smiled, so Yusif smiled back and pointed over at the guardian angels, as he knew the child could see them as well. The child's gaze returned to the group by the counter, chatting with the angels. His mother took hold of him by the hand and pulled him away, to continue on their journey down the street. The small boy tried to break free, all the while, looking back towards the café, trying to pull away in protest of being forced away from the visage, but her grip was too strong and she pulled him back. Eventually his objection fell away and he then happily continued on his way, with his family.

Yusif could see the young child's guardian angel, who waved at him as he sat there in the café, so Yusif smiled and waved back. Both Yusif and the angel knew that what the child had seen, would stay with him for the rest of his life. The guardian angel of the boy sent Yusif a telepathic message that he had only slightly revealed himself to the child; that slowly he would reveal more of himself to the child, as he grew older. Once the child was of age he would reveal himself fully. For now, little glimpses would be enough, as a way of piquing the child's interest.

Yusif turned back around in his chair, so that he was once again, facing straight ahead and watching the conversation between Paul, Sara and Mariyah continue.

"I have felt this presence around me before, only not as strong," admitted Mariyah.

Paul explained that her guardian angels had been waiting for the moment when they could step forward and let her see and feel their presence.

"Was that you I felt around me when I was crying and upset about a month ago?" Asked Mariyah.

"Yes, that was us. We have been with you since your birth into the physical world. We have always been with you. Even before your birth we were with you," said one of them.

Mariyah could hear them clearly speaking to her inside her head. "A few years ago, a voice once said to me, 'one day you will work for God'. Was that you too?" She asked.

"Yes, we were planting seeds to keep you from becoming one of those who hear not. We see you are now ready to move on. You have been through the Earthly lessons, now we want to take you, show you and teach you about life beyond the Earthly plane. We are here to work with you, to help you in your learning and development. You are now of age and ready to learn if you so wish," said the guardian angel.

With all this beautiful loving energy flowing through Mariyah, she could not help but burst into tears. It was a beautiful moment in her life, a real revelation of truth, she had been waiting for. Since speaking to Paul and Sara, Mariyah's mental state had drastically changed. She was able to remove all hidden doubts that had previously created conflicting beliefs within her. Once Mariyah's tears had dried up, Paul and Sara explained to her how to connect to her guardian angels through meditation. Yusif watched, as a beautiful pink light energy completely fill the whole café.

"God has arranged for someone in the physical world to help you. She will be able to teach you how to become more aware of the hereafter. Each person's journey is one that will eventually lead them to seeking the home of the hereafter. Your real journey is about to begin. Remain working here for a while. One who works for us will come into the café and you will serve her. From there you will strike up a conversation and it will be as if you have known each other your whole lives," Sara explained and Mariyah's light energy began to expand again as she filled with happiness. The last five minutes of the conversation was filled with more tears from Mariyah. She wiped her eyes and gave both of them a hug. She was now full of smiles and laughter. She looked over at Yusif and gave him a wave. Yusif waved back with a smile, as he sat there wondering what Paul, Sara and her guardian angels had spoken to her about. Shortly afterwards, Paul and Sara returned to the table.

"Everything is now fine," said Sara, as she sat down.

"It was so beautiful to watch this moment, when someone truly awakens to the reality of the spiritual world and the heavy load is lifted from their mind," said Yusif, as he moved over to let Paul sit down.

"That is why I love this work," said Paul, as he straightened his clothing.

Sara agreed and smiled because she too, would not want to do any other kind of work, other than what she is doing.

"While you were talking to Mariyah, a small boy looked through the window and he saw you speaking with the guardian angels. What a day this has been. Truly, this has been one of the best days of my life and it has been an honour and a blessing bestowed on me. I also thank you, Paul and Sara, it has been an honour," said Yusif, with a smiled.

"We can all agree on that, it has been an honour and a privilege," said Paul.

Mariyah came over to the table. Her guardian angels followed her. She was still wiping her eyes where the tears had left a wet trail.

"Thank you, thank you, thank you," gushed Mariyah.

In fact, she would not stop saying it. Paul and Sara assured her that it was all part of their work. Her guardian angels told her that they would be returning to see her, however, if ever she needed them, to just call out to them and they would be with her in an instant. They whispered their names into her ear and then they slowly faded away.

Mariyah returned to her seat by the side of the counter where she packed away her food boxes in order to resume her work. Mariyah began to serve some new customers that had walked into the café. Paul and Sara told Yusif that Mariyah was a very special and spiritual young woman. They told him that Mariyah had experienced many extremely beautiful, spiritual experiences but because she did not have anyone to help her make sense of them, she thought that she was going crazy. Paul and Sara were able to give her some guidance and understanding about her experiences and what she could expect going forward now that she had met her guardian angels. Paul and Sara explained that through meditation, she would be able to connect and receive direct guidance. It would happen slowly at first, but as she developed, the guidance would increase, encouraging Mariyah to meditate often, which would strengthen the link between herself and her guardian angels.

"The best way to connect to them, is through love and, listening to that which comes through her higher self. She will then become one of those who are rightly guided." Said Paul.

Yusif looked over at Mariyah again and he could see the loving feelings within her, radiating in every direction. It was like switching on a light, he realised that before this moment, the world had caused Mariyah to contain her divine, inner expression of love, placing great limitations on her, as a spiritual human being. Now she could start to live her life, without the constraints her doubts had imposed on her. She was now free to explore and expand her immediate consciousness awareness. He could also see that she had an amazing intelligence which exceeded many of those around her. She would use her intelligence and vision to explain to others what she feels and learns from her guardian angels. Mariyah still had a number of physical world experiences that would challenge her, yet at the same time strengthen her. It was sent to Yusif, as inspiration, that she would see cracks appear in the foundations she had created as a safety net. At first, the cracks would appear small and hardly noticeable, however, those cracks would grow bigger. She had to learn not to doubt what was in front of her, to follow her intuition, think about what others denied and refuse to deny it to herself. She would have to make a choice and decide how best to rebuild a new foundation for her and her family. She would eventually realise that building a family based on old family ideals, would not be the best way forward to build her own family for the future. This would mean that she would have to make some difficult decisions about where her family grew up.

Mariyah came over to the table. "Is there anything else I can do for you?" She asked.

"No, we are fine, but thank you for asking. It's time for us to leave," said Paul.

Paul and Sara stood up and started walking toward the back door of the café, but as Yusif moved to follow them, he began to feel the strange sensation of butterflies in his stomach. At first, he thought it might have been caused by the food he had eaten, but Paul and Sara seemed fine, so he let the thought go and continued on to catch up with them at the exit to the café. He caught the faint glimmer, of a female brushing past him which caused him to become immediately overwhelmed by an instantaneous recognition of a deep love, that connected him to this female. This, he realised, was the very moment he had been waiting for, for much of his adult life. He was completely taken aback by the unfamiliar feelings he was experiencing, as though he knew something but couldn't quite grasp it, or like when you have words on the tip of your tongue and you cannot think how to say it. This was one of those moments.

I wonder what her name is? Yusif asked himself. He knew he knew it but was unable to remember or recall it, so he called out to Paul and Sara, who were almost out of the exit.

"Help me out here?" Yusif pleaded, causing Paul and Sara to turn around.

Without Yusif needing to pose the question, Sara smiled and said, "Ah yes, a soul's consciousness can travel ahead of time. It is part of the connections that are made between people. Most people are unaware of these connections that are made in advance..." she explained.

"Made in advance of what?" Yusif asked.

Instead of answering Yusif's question, Paul and Sara turned back toward the exit and left, leaving Yusif confused and a little frustrated because he did not quite understand what Sara had said and his mind was racing in all different directions, trying to think of the name of the female that he had encountered. He took a few steps to follow the phantom, but the already faint figure faded away. Yusif was left speechless as she disappeared from his sight. Not knowing why he would be compelled to look down at the ground, rather than follow Paul and Sara, he did and saw a beautifully crafted silver bracelet with thirteen different coloured gemstones embedded into it. He bent down to pick it up, hoping to have a physical reminder of this person, or something he could return to her, should their paths cross again, in either the physical or spiritual plane, however, only inches from his fingers, it also began to fade. Looking around, Yusif realised she and the bracelet were gone from his awareness. However, the image of the bracelet was now etched in his mind.

A few of the customers in the café were looking in his direction with puzzled looks and of course, he realised that they did not have the same awareness he had and wouldn't know what he was doing or why he was asking such a question of his friends, about a female who was not there.

So, he followed Paul and Sara, making his way down the small passageway to the exit. He was suddenly blinded by a light that appeared to surround him and when he re-opened his eyes, he found himself in the hallway of his home, with a letter in his hand.

He stood there, bewildered for a moment, looking at the letter, still trying to piece together the events that had just taken place in the café. He wanted to get back there to speak with the female he had encountered. Nothing seemed to be making sense, flitting between locations, strange feelings, unexpected encounters, seemingly alone, without Paul and Sara guiding him, he also noticed that his bodily manifestation felt lighter again; he was once again, back in his spiritual body. Jolting him out of his reverie, the doorbell rang, so he hurried over to answer the door, none too gracefully as he tripped over himself and knocked over a small table with a book on it. He picked up the book and put it back on the table. He reached out towards the door handle and as he made contact with it, just as he was about to open the door, he found himself returned to the company of Paul and Sara, all of them now standing in front of the teleportation crystals, from where they had started this journey.

"Yusif, are you feeling alright?" Paul asked, getting no response, so he called out to Yusif again, only this time a little louder, "YUSIF! Are you feeling alright?" While also putting his hand on Yusif's shoulder and looking into his eyes.

Yusif looked at Paul. He was feeling a little unsteady on his legs, a little fluttery in the stomach, after the experience in the café, disorientated of being in his home and now back in the crystal structure.

"What? Huh?" Yusif mumbled, as he stared at Paul and then at Sara, in a bit of a confused way. It took him a while to get his bearings.

Paul beckoned for him to sit down for a moment, which he did. After a short rest and a drink of water, Yusif returned to being fully back and aware. He stood up and they left the transporter room. Questions were running around in Yusif's mind, but he could not formulate them into words. In the end, he kept silent about the two final experiences in the café and his home. All he had was this image of the bracelet on the floor of the café before it disappeared. Now that Yusif was feeling himself again and he had recovered after the journey to his home city of Bradford, he realised it was time to say goodbye to Paul and Sara. He still had one more task to complete.

He had stood by and watched others complete the tasks that they had been given. It was now time for him to make the journey to the island of lost souls. He would have to make the journey alone. He knew he would have to use all the experience and wisdom he had learnt while he was a visitor in the hereafter.

Yusif was re-joined by his companions and they left the crystal structure. They continued their journey across the lake to the island. His companions reminded him that all things happen and manifest for a reason. This made Yusif feel happier and he was able to return to the here and now.

Yusif's companions continued to teach him about what happens when you pass over from the physical world. They explained many things, such as, when a soul leaves the Earth plane, its adjustment to a life in the spiritual world is dependent on its spiritual awareness and understanding and on leaving the physical world, the majority of souls are met by loved ones. At first, when the soul arrives in the hereafter, they still have certain cravings as they did in the physical world. Eating and sleeping, are not the needs of the spiritual self. Without the body, these needs quickly fade away. Physical illnesses and lost limbs remain with the physical body. The only disease a spirit can carry over from the physical world into the hereafter, is only its own negative expression. If there is a lot of focused concentration on a particular image or events, the spirit can become surrounded and locked within it, as a recurring event. These images are created out of an experience in the physical world. Problems can arise for the soul when they are unable to let the moment go. The light can become darkness if the soul becomes transfixed on too much negative emotion. While on Earth, souls should strive to be the best they can. Love and its expression will always bring out the best within. Through the spirit of inspiration, comes the best construction of the truth to guide you.

"All souls become aware that they have to review their life and deeds when they arrive in the hereafter. Using the detailed record of their deeds which misses nothing out, the review that takes place is an important part of their learning. It is something all souls must attend to. It is with love, that their account against themselves, is reviewed. They see how their actions affected others in the life of the world. With this new understanding, there is a shift in their thinking and duty towards others. Through it, they are able to start putting right their record. For some, their own shame creates fear and they refuse to come to the light. They refuse the help of their friends or guardian angel. Their conditioning has taught them to fear God in the wrong way. The companions also reminded Yusif that certain freedoms are still granted to souls in the hereafter, but if a soul refuses to be of service, the energy that manifests, will transport the soul to a place in the lower regions of the Heavens. Only through service will a soul be invited to live in the best of Heavens. Surrendering to the loving truth is the best kind of surrender. Irregularities within the soul lead to numerous disorders. One of those is the refusal to surrender. The second one is a refusal to review the record about the deeds they did during their Earthly life. A wall can start to build around them like a partition when they reject the inner truth. The collected darkness forms a partition of rejected ideas that hems them in. They can take that rejection with them into the hereafter." One companion explained.

"When a person cannot see beyond what is in front of them, meditation will allow them to break down what is there, into small, manageable pieces. They will then be able to deal with the matter a little bit at a time. They will become wise about when the irregularities start to rise within them as they cycle around their polarity. Each soul peels away bits of their own darkness. It will eventually become subdued and then dissolve completely." A second companion continued.

"Let meditation help you to break down that which arises. As it dissolves, you will see beyond what is manifesting around you. You must strive to see beyond that which blocks your view. The benefits are many, but as many as they are, most of humanity is led astray by the life of the world and its glitter. With clarity restored to their vision about why the lessons happened in their life, they are able to move beyond the event." The companions took turns to enlighten Yusif with their wisdom.

"For those enraged, there is no quick way for them to change their state of being. Each soul must reap what it has sown and is justly dealt with. Listen to your greater self. You will then be of those who strive to become the best of their efforts. Those who express love and meditate, work to maintain their spiritual connection and rise above the conditions that surround them. Meditation greatly helps the soul on its arrival in the hereafter."

Yusif was fascinated by the experiences and understanding he was gaining. He already understood some of the things they were speaking about, however, when those same things were spoken about and explained to him in the hereafter, the words reached deep inside of him. There was such an air of truth in the hereafter; that which was said, could not be denied. Yusif realised that it is the recognition of truth that touches the inner soul. Only the truth is revealed and spoken by those in the greater states of the hereafter. They speak only according to the divine flow of the spirit of inspiration. As they continued their journey across the water, apprehensive thoughts began to enter Yusif's mind.

THE LAND OF SHADOWS

In the distance, Yusif could see the outline of an island and hovering above it dark clouds, yet some way off, they all came to a stop, floating above the lake.

"We can go no further," said one of the companions.

"Before you go, visualise a bubble of protection around yourself. Take the crystal from the bag and look within it. Let it take you to the part of the island you need to be," explained another companion.

No sooner had Yusif created the intention and looked at the image of the island in the crystal, he found himself standing on the island's beach. It was not what he expected at all. He looked from side to side and then turned around. Looking out over the lake, his companions were nowhere to be seen.

That was quick, Yusif thought to himself.

Looking around, he felt he had not had enough time to really prepare himself. It was the going from one extreme to another, in a matter of seconds, that startled Yusif. The island had an uncomfortable feeling about it. Even the music Earl had been inspired to compose, was silent. All he could hear was a low, vibrational humming. Yusif thought that if Earl had created this humming vibration around the island, there was a good reason. The feeling of loneliness and despair was all around. The island was in semidarkness due to the dark clouds overhead, yet visibility was still quite good. He opened his hand and looked at the crystal, a little disappointed and worried as it was no longer radiating its light. It was now a darker colour that had taken on the appearance and expression of the island. Yusif stared into the crystal and saw a faint flicker of light, like the twinkling of a star on a cloudy night. He looked around again, wondering what he should do.

How quickly things can change. He thought to himself.

Yusif felt a resistance as he tried to reach out with his awareness and see beyond the decay, realising it had become limited. Everything he had learnt during his life did not help improve his perception and awareness about the island. It was from this point a darkness within him started to manifest and he even began to feel a little nervous, as he took in his surroundings. He decided to hide the crystal; he could come back for it once he had discovered what to do with it. As he started walking from the water's edge, up the beach, he passed a collection of stones, some were lying flat and others standing upright.

Were these rock crystals at one time? He wondered.

He noticed a tree stump at the edge of an embankment where the top part of the tree had broken off through decayed and had fallen over under the weight of its branches. He decided this would be a good place to hide the crystal, as it was from a tree stump that he had originally been given the crystal. He looked into the top of the hollowed-out stump, to see a soft, muddy substance. He knew the crystal was very precious, so he decided to place it on top of the mud and cover it with a couple of handfuls of sand. He gently placed it on top of the mud and was about to get some sand to cover it over, when it started to sink into the mud of its own accord.

"NO! NO!" Yusif yelled, as he watched it sink down and disappear under the soft, muddy sand, hoping he would still be able to retrieve it when the time came.

There are not many people who would put their hands in there, he thought to himself, as the crystal became fully submerged in a matter of moments. *Why would they want to put their hands in there, or even know the crystal was there?* He thought, resignedly shrugging his shoulders.

Yusif walked to the top of a small embankment and gazed in all directions, looking or waiting for inspiration, to help him decide his next steps. As he looked to his right, he could see an object that looked like a rock crystal. It stood three to four feet in height but was slightly different from the rocks on the beach at the island.

Mm, maybe it has not been here as long? He said to himself, as he walked towards it.

He wiped away the dirt, cleaning it the best he could, revealing a rock crystal that was violet in colour. Yusif remembered the seven small crystal orbs that Earl had given him in the studio. Taking the small bag from the larger bag holding the crystal, he opened it and tipped the contents into his hand. One of the crystal orbs was the same colour as the violet crystal in front of him. Without conscious knowledge of why he would do this, he placed the small, violet crystal orb on top of the rock crystal and watched as it was absorbed into the larger one. It moved downwards inside the rock crystal and about halfway down it came to a stop, just hanging there, floating, as if it were suspended in time and space. After only a few seconds, a small light flickered inside the rock crystal. Yusif peered into it and recognised that the flickering light was actually a symbol, which quickly faded away, but seemed to be the catalyst for the rock crystal to send out a pulse of energy, only then to return to its natural violet colour. Yusif remained squatting in front of the violet rock crystal, recalling the conversation he had with Earl back in the studio, how Earl had been inspired to infuse each crystal orb with a symbol. *Was that inspiration sent to Earl to unknowingly aid Yusif in his quest?* Yusif pondered.

Yusif stood from his crouching position and looked down at the sand and debris he'd left behind when he cleaned the violet rock crystal and he noticed a few pieces of wood, that he knew were not there when he first approached the rock crystal. They were all laid out neatly in the form of an arrow, which pointed toward some kind of pathway. He followed the embankment to where the pathway started, and made his way along the track, well if you could call it a track. It was more of a bumpy track that animals would use as they headed towards new pastures. He followed the thin line of the track as it wound its way towards the edge of a forest. Although most of the land was in a state of decay, there were some small patches of greenery. Yusif was not sure what to expect during his time on the island, so he stopped at the edge of the forest, wondering if it was safe to enter. His decision was to push on, so he could complete the task and return to the land he had left. He entered the forest and could hear the rustling and creaking of the branches and leaves, as the wind moved them back and forth. All that had grown had lost its colour, further confirming that the whole place was in a state of decay. Yusif was in a state of bewilderment, as he mumbled to himself about his present situation. He could sense the decay of this land mingling with his own fears, but he pushed the negative thoughts aside, so that he could think more clearly about the direction he needed to travel to accomplish the quest.

As time passed, Yusif knew that he had not travelled that far, yet he began to feel drained and a little exhausted from journeying, so he sat on a rock for a rest. As he looked back along the track, he started to reflect on some of the things from his past. He once again entered the time when he was at school, during which time he had been bullied, realising that this was probably the main reason he avoided being in the company of other people. He had even refused to participate in some activities, not because he did not really want to take part, but because he felt awkward in the company of others.

As his negative emotions grew and rushed to the forefront of his mind, like a stampede of wild animals, his failures came rushing forth. In this state of mind, he recalled thoughts and situations that he did not even realise had existed within. For a moment, he forgot about the quest and questioned his own self-worth. He looked up to see dark manifestations appearing and realised that he was creating them because of the thoughts and situations he was reflecting on. He snapped himself out of this mindset, after he realised, he was becoming consumed. It was the words of wisdom spoken by the Crilarian, when he first came to the beach, which helped him to refocus on his task.

"Focus, focus," he said to himself, in a low voice, as he got up from sitting on the rock. He followed the track, walking slowly at first, as he began to shift his focus of attention back onto the task and quest at hand. As he continued through the forest, he came across a clearing, in the centre of which stood a similar-shaped rock crystal to the one at the top of the embankment. This one had an indigo colour to it. Again, he cleaned the rock crystal and looked around to see if there were any instructions to help him on his journey, which he didn't see, so he decided to repeat what he had done at the violet rock crystal. He pulled out his bag of crystal orbs, selected the indigo coloured one and placed it at the top of the large rock crystal. Like the first one, it merged and descended down through the rock crystal and came to a stop. It began to radiate a small symbol of light and then faded away, followed by emitting a pulse of energy, before returning to its original colour. Yusif glanced at the ground around the rock crystal and sure enough, there was that arrow, this time made of tree branches showing him the direction he should go. Yusif recognised there was a pattern to the tasks he was performing, that they were leading him (hopefully) in the right direction and he assumed he would find a blue rock crystal next, if his logic were correct. As Yusif looked in the direction the arrow pointed, he mentally created a pathway he could take, but then he remembered the special crystal he had left on the beach and wanted to be sure he could find his way back to retrieve it. So, he started to climb the nearest tree, hoping that when he reached the top, he would be able to see the beach and lodge its direction in his memory. He reached up to the next level branch, to pull himself higher, to get a better view of the path he had already taken and that would take him back to the beach, when he heard a snapping sound. The branch had broken off, causing him to fall back to the ground. Shocked but uninjured, he got back on his feet and started the climb again. He climbed high enough to be able to look back at the way he had come; when unbidden into his mind, the thought came that he would surely lose sight of his goal, if he let himself become absorbed by the struggles of the past. Climbing back down the tree, Yusif decided to move on, leaving behind the path that he had travelled. He focused on the direction taking him forward, as this gave him meaning and purpose.

Yusif travelled along the track that wound its meandering way through the forest, the terrain harder than Yusif thought it would be, with swerving routes and bumpy, lumpy ground, causing him more than once to lose his balance or twist an ankle, as he tried to navigate it as best he could. Even when he could see a tricky part of the path ahead of him, he still managed to slip and fall. He rolled down an embankment and over some dense bushes. Sharp thorns found a way through his clothing and the pain they caused shattered his stability of mind and he fell into desperate despair. He just laid there, where he had stopped, feeling utterly defeated, to the point where he took in a good few deep breaths and shouted out loudly, "AAAHHHH!" His frustration heard clearly in his voice.

He was annoyed with himself that he'd slipped and fell, scraping both his palms and knees, which were stinging now. He tried to put together the fragmented memories of the beautiful place that he had left but it seemed far from where he was now.

He got to his knees and was about to stand up, when he saw something through the trees, a group of darkened figures in the distance. He remembered what he was told, that there were some lost souls on the island and it would appear that these grey figures with elongated mouths and torn, grey, straggly clothing, were some of the souls trapped in this land. Yusif hid behind a tree, watching as the figures looked around. They started to push and shove each other back and forth, they were arguing, bickering and almost fighting among themselves but after a while they moved off in another direction and Yusif was glad to see the back of them. He reckoned they had appeared because he cried out.

If they fight like that among themselves, what would they do to me? He thought to himself.

Yusif quietly moved off, not wanting to alert or see those lost souls again. A short while later he came across the next rock crystal in a circular clearing in the middle of the forest and as expected, this one was blue. He followed the same process as before, by getting the blue crystal orb from the bag and placing it on the top of the rock crystal. This too was absorbed to its mid-way point, where the sacred symbol flashed and then faded, before it sent out its pulse of energy and returned to its normal blue colour. Yusif expected another arrow to appear which would, once again, point him in the right direction and he was not disappointed. However, this arrow had been etched into a large rock, along with the instruction to: 'keep following the arrows,' also carved into the rock. Yusif felt a kind of peace settling over him, as he took a moment to look around, feeling confident he was following the right path to reach his journey's end and complete his quest. He stood still for a moment listening to the sound of silence, broken only by the natural creaking and rustling of the forest.

Yusif moved off in the direction the arrow pointed, adjusting his garments after the fall and with an increased determination to press on. He had been walking on this forest path for, what felt like, quite some time and because the pathway was a winding one, he was beginning to feel a little lost, so he made an educated guess about the direction he should take. After a while, he began to see things that were not there. The shapes of the trees were beginning to play tricks with his mind. He even stopped a couple of times and hid because he thought he saw something. When this had happened a few times, he began to laugh at himself, for creating fears that did not exist. This did make him feel better about himself and the forest that surrounded him.

Yusif heard thunder rolling above him and so he looked up to see dark clouds building up rapidly over the island. He got the sinking feeling that the land he was in, did not want him to leave, putting obstacles in his way and its determination to hold him back, seemed to be building up to match his own equally determined desire to succeed. Yusif could feel every part of himself straining to stay focused and retain a consistency of thought. In his mind, he found himself continually striving to mentally push himself, in a bid to stay focused and see beyond the decay of the island.

There was another crash of thunder overhead, but Yusif remained positive, he was still alive and as long as he was alive, the completion of the task was still on. He took a few deep breaths making him feel more relaxed, while also knowing that if he rested, even for a moment, he would lose the pace he had built up. Finally, ahead, he could see another rock crystal, in a clearing within the forest. Finding this crystal was a relief, as it confirmed he was still traveling in the right direction. He approached the rock crystal to see that it was lying on its side and he thought the merging of the crystal orb might not work properly if it wasn't upright, so he decided to do just that, put it in the right position.

"One, two and three," he counted out loud, as he attempted to lift the rock crystal.

It was quite heavy and it took him a few attempts to lift it. The impact from when the rock crystal had landed had caused it to fall over. It had obviously been a stumbling block for the other souls that had come to the island to attempt this quest as they had not managed to lift it into its correct position. Once it was upright and steady (Yusif having packed one side of its crater with soil and normal rocks, to stop it falling over again) the green-coloured rock crystal glowed and sent out a pulse of energy that moved through the trees, causing them to slightly sway. He took out the bag of crystal orbs but couldn't find one that matched or complimented the green of the rock crystal. Not sure what to do about this deviation from the process he had followed previously, he decided to try each one of them in turn, to see if any of them worked. The first stone sat there, balanced on top and did absolutely nothing, so he tried another one with the same result. At this point, he was becoming worried that he wouldn't be able to complete his quest, if he didn't get the next arrow to give him the new direction to follow.

"Let's hope Earl had not forgotten to put all the crystals I needed in the bag, before he gave them to me," Yusif said to himself.

It was not until he put the pink crystal orb onto the rock crystal, that anything happened and Yusif was both relieved as he saw it begin to descend, as the others had, but also worried that it was the wrong colour and might give unexpected results. A pink glow appeared and swirled around inside, the sacred symbol appeared and faded away and the rock crystal emitted its energy pulse, just as the others had. He waited for a moment, watching to see if anything else would happen and slowly the light of the larger crystal faded. Yusif looked closer and could see a faint pink light within it. At the base of the rock crystal there was a line of branches on the ground. It was not an arrow but could have been an arrow at one time. It was his only clue, so he decided to follow the way it appeared to be pointed.

Yusif had not gone far, when a large group of grey figures appeared and began looking around. They had obviously detected the pulse of energy that was sent out from the rock crystal when Yusif had stood it upright. As he watched them moving through the forest, he could see that they were beginning to close in on him. He managed crawl away and lose them, but they suddenly reappeared directly ahead of him. They looked directly at him. He knew he could not hide, so he stood there while he thought about what to do next. He did not want to turn back as he knew this would open the door of his mind to whatever fear existed. He was determined to focus on going forward. Turning back in fear would stay with him for the rest of his life. He did not want to live with that kind of regret. He knew he had to push on through, no matter what. On either side of the group were rocks and thick bushes. Having experienced the pain of trying to rush through that kind of terrain before, he knew it was not a good option and it would drastically slow him down. If he fell or stumbled as he had before, the grey figures would easily overwhelm him, if he became trapped and there were more of them this time. He continued to watch them, as they watched him, they conversed with one another, becoming argumentative, as they squabbled between themselves as to who would claim him. Yusif saw that the grey figures did not appear to be solid and he knew that his best hopes of getting past them, was to not let any fears hold him back, so he decided to take his chances and run straight through them. He knew that if he moved quickly, they would not be able to stop him. He waited for the right opportunity and it wasn't long in coming, as a fight broke out among them. This left only a couple to focus on what Yusif was doing. This was his opportunity.

He set off running. They were not expecting him to run towards them and by the time they realised what he was doing, Yusif was moving at quite a speed, directly towards them. He passed quite a few of them before they realised what was happening. Those within reach stretched out their hands to catch him and Yusif could feel their spikey fingers brushing over him as they tried to grab hold of him. His focus allowed him to maintain his strength of mind and his determination drove him forward. His quick thinking, weaving and dodging, made it difficult for them to block his way or hold him back. Their faces became more terrifying as they tried to scare him into submission. He cried out in anger at himself, as he fought to hold his concentration and not give in to the fear that began to fill him. He knew that the fear within him was but a state of mind and states of mind can quickly change. He had now entered into a self-preservation mind-set and from within him a small light force pulsated out, which pushed the figures back a few feet. After a few quick steps and a bit of ducking and diving, he was past them. They gave chase but after hiding and dodging from tree to tree, he managed to lose them again.

He could now continue his journey with relative ease. The fear that Yusif had felt a few moments before, quickly faded and had now grown into self-confidence. He realised that if he could overcome fear, he could deal with any situation. The way he dealt with the lost souls, instilled a positive mental mind-set. He was feeling much more confident.

Relieved to be free of the shadow figures and slowing his pace to catch his breath back, Yusif continued his journey through the forest, until he came upon another clearing, in the centre of which stood a yellow rock crystal. He could tell by the size of the impact area, where the crystal landed, that it had released quite a bit of energy, when it arrived. Many trees around it were lying on their sides or were leaning at an angle. He looked around as he made his way over to the crystal to clean it. When he looked into the crystal, he saw images of each crystal's impact, as they landed.

This explains the clearings around the crystals. He thought to himself, as he looked at the trees slanting to the side.

The impact and the energy released by the rock crystal's landings, had awoken some of the tree spirits from their hibernation. The damage caused to the trees had forced them from their homes. They were not happy. The trees were too badly damaged for them to return to. At least Yusif knew who and what he was dealing with in the forest; they were the lost souls of the tree spirits, abruptly forced to look for new, uninhabited trees to dwell in, but of course, there weren't any available, as the trees that were upright, already had a tree spirit dwelling within them. Yusif could understand their frustration and fear, but unfortunately he could not offer them any solace or solutions – he had his quest to complete right now – but afterwards, if he was to meet his companions again, he made a mental note to tell them about the problem, to see if they could do anything to help, before the souls were lost forever. With his quest in mind, Yusif added the yellow crystal orb to the rock crystal and set off again in the direction the new arrow pointed.

As he walked, Yusif thought some more about the gentle tree spirit he had seen in Bakka, earlier on his journey and decided that these tree spirits seemed to have an opposite demeanour. These were angry and understandably so, but why would they want to attack him? He was not responsible for the damage done to their homes.

Yusif heard a commotion coming from somewhere in the forest around him, so he looked through the trees trying to identify the source of the commotion. To his left, in the distance and thankfully, not in the direction he needed to travel, he saw a large number of the tree spirits congregating and soon the general commotion turned into the sound of a large group chanting. He started walking quickly, to put some distance between the sound and himself. He did not want to wait around to find out why they were gathering. He knew it would not be for any good cause.

He continued his journey through the forest and the sound of the chanting faded away for a while, giving Yusif some relief, thinking the tree spirits had not detected his presence. However, just a few minutes later he started to pick up on a humming sound. At first, he thought it was the distant chanting of the tree spirits, coming back into his sphere of perception and that meant they were coming in his direction again. Feeling disappointed, Yusif set off at a jog, to try and create a larger gap between them, to avoid them, if at all possible, but he realised that the sound he was hearing was actually different and not a chant at all. As the sound got louder, he compared it to the sounds made in the crystal structure, when he was with Earl in the music studio, so he decided to investigate it further.

Yusif changed his direction of travel slightly, being drawn towards the source of the humming, as it increased in volume and clarity. Through the trees, he could see a large clearing in the forest, thinking it might be another rock crystal site, he headed towards it but as he got closer to the edge of the clearing, his foot wouldn't touch down to the floor and, as his other foot left the ground to follow, he started to rise into the air, as if there was no gravity in this place to keep him anchored. He quickly grabbed hold of a tree, to halt his elevation and manoeuvred himself around the clearing, pushing himself from tree to tree. Yusif was finding it extremely difficult to stay close to the ground and he knew instinctively, that if he let go of the trees, he would float upwards, potentially never being able to come back down. This prompted him to look up into the sky, where he was surprised to see some large rocks; they looked like floating mountains in the air. There was one large rock and two smaller rocks, about half the size of the bigger one and although these floating rocks were not as large as the structures on the lake, there did seem to be a resemblance. He could also see a shimmering effect that encircled the area where the rocks were floating. He decided not to venture into this area. The only thing that was stopping him from floating up to them was his hold on the trees near the edge of the clearing. Looking across the clearing for the final time, he could see that hundreds of trees were lying on their sides, many of which looked as though they had been crushed by something very large, which also meant that there would be hundreds of displaced and angry tree spirits, wandering around and Yusif was glad he had not encountered them yet.

Yusif looked up again at the floating mountains, knowing he would not be able to come back down to the ground if he tried to venture beyond the shimmering effect. Yusif thought about the singing bowls back in Earl's studio. *Were these the rocks Earl had spoken about during his time in the structure on the lake?* There was no rock crystal in the centre of the clearing as Yusif had been expecting, so Yusif knew this was not the correct path or direction, so he returned to the forest, away from the humming, to where his feet could be planted firmly back on the ground. He then continued his journey, looking for another way.

Transforming the Island

Yusif had been walking quite a while and eventually, the trees around him started to thin out. He was relieved that he had definitely been going in the right direction because he'd found the sixth rock crystal, this time orange in colour and it did not need to be cleaned. He retrieved one of the two remaining crystal orbs given to him by Earl and placed it on top of the crystal, where it disappeared inside, flashed the sacred symbol and emitted its energy pulse. A set of stones in the shape of an arrow appeared on the ground, giving Yusif his next direction to follow. Reaching the edge of the trees, a flicker of light caught his attention and he could see a lone figure sitting on a rock at the edge of the trees. It was not another rock crystal and the figure was not like any of the other ones he had encountered earlier, as this one had a detectable life force, but it had grown dim. Yusif decided that rather than engage with this figure, as he had initially with the tree spirits, he would make all haste to complete his journey and quest, so he crouched down low, alternating glances between the figure and his destination direction, to be sure that the figure hadn't noticed him. The arrow for his new direction pointed across a barren patch of land, which wouldn't give him good cover for stealth. It was bare of trees and all that he could see were some patches of grass and shrubbery surrounded by dried out, cracked soil. It looked like, at one time, it might have been grassland. In the distance, he noticed three large hills, each of them rising to a rounded point. He could sense a pathway that would lead from this land, between two of the hills and figured this must be his new destination.

Despite Yusif's decision to avoid the figure sitting on the rock, his curiosity got the better of him. *What was that flicker of life-force he had seen around the figure, and why had it dimmed?* He thought to himself. He watched in puzzlement as the figure would run in the direction of the hills, but a dense fog that had faces appearing in it, materialised on every attempt he made and this forced the figure to retreat, back to his rock at the tree boundary. Small flickers of light would dance about the figure, seeming to revitalise it, giving it strength for another try. Yusif started to move in closer, to see if he could make out who the figure was and as he did, he could detect a strong, masculine, energy signature coming from the figure, however, Yusif's focus was broken by a crash of thunder, as it rolled across the heavens. Yusif looked behind him in the direction of the forest and through the trees, where he could see a build-up of a dark mass, growing larger by the minute. His senses told him that the lost souls were gathering, in an attempt to overwhelm both the figure and himself. A streak of lightning struck the ground, not far from Yusif, which made him stand up and set off running. He stopped in the open space beyond the edge of the trees and the dark fog coalesced around him. He fanatically waved his hands around, trying to dissipate the fog, when suddenly his friend Paul appeared some distance from the fog, which distracted the fog's inhabitants for a moment, allowing Yusif to break free and get away. Yusif realised that the fog was only the thought manifestations of the tree spirits; *they did not or could not really harm him, could they?* They had accumulated into a dark and foggy mass over time, from the negative energy sent out by the tree spirits. The fog moved towards Paul, however, before the entities inhabiting the fog could get to him, he disappeared.

The figure that was sitting on the rock was now looking in Yusif's direction.

"RUN!" Yusif shouted and they took off in the direction of the hillside.

After a while, Yusif glanced back in the direction of the

figure. He could see he was falling behind, so he shouted words of encouragement, to keep him running. The dark fog with the faces started to pursue them, as they made their way towards the hillside.

It was not long before the mysterious figure began breathing heavily, eventually coming to a stop and bending over, with his hands resting on his knees, trying to get his breath back. The figure's energy began to dull, with some areas turning grey. Yusif could see he was totally exhausted, as the figure looked in his direction, his despair clear to sense and though Yusif could still see the small light projecting from the figure, it looked like it also was diminishing. Yusif received inspiration then, that this was happening to the figure because of the fear he was manifesting, it was soaking up the light energy that would normally provide some revitalisation. The figure was reaching out with what strength he had and Yusif remembered his time on Earth with Paul and Sara, how some souls could share their energy with others. Closing his eyes, Yusif focused. He visualised a light projecting from himself that went out and surrounded the figure. As the light surrounded the exhausted figure, it created an immediate healing, that gave the figure more energy and renewed strength. The reason Yusif had more energy than the figure was all thanks to his grandfather, who had taught Yusif to protect a greater part of his mind from the darkness that tried to invade it. He also remembered about the need for protection Paul and Sara had taught him. This allowed him to maintain a stronger than usual mindset. A positive mental attitude acted like a shield and stopped vital energy being drained. His mental attitude was also part of the protection he used to create a barrier that stopped his thoughts swerving. Yusif opened his eyes to see the figure was now standing straight. Sparks of radiating light flickered all around the figure. Turning, they both set off running again, in the direction of the hillside.

Yusif was the first to arrive at the passageway between two hills. He looked back to see the figure was still radiating light, so he shouted more words of encouragement. Following a short track between the two hillsides, he came across the seventh rock crystal, which was red in colour. He wiped it down and placed the last of the crystal orbs,

Earl had given him, on top. Now that Yusif had used all the crystal orbs, he stepped back, waiting for something to happen. The red rock crystal glowed, sent out a small pulse and then returned to its original colour and brightness.

Come on, Yusif said to himself.

He expected something more to happen once he had put the last of the crystal orbs in place. He reflected over the journey and was not sure what else he could have done. He had placed all the seven crystal orbs on top of the rock crystals. Each one had its own symbol that energised the crystal. They had all lit up and sent out a small pulse of energy. He began to doubt and wondered if he had missed some vital step along the way. He put the small empty bag back into the larger bag where the strap looped over his head and the bag hung by his side.

Unknown to Yusif, when the last of the crystal orbs was in place, all the orbs glowed at the same time and the rock crystal he had hidden in the log on the beach, suddenly began to grow in size. The trunk surrounding the rock crystal had decayed so much, that as the rock crystal grew, it split the wood. The rock crystal established itself in the ground and was standing four feet in height. A small orb of multiple colours began to swirl around inside the rock crystal, as it waited to be activated.

Yusif continued on past the red rock crystal, along the pathway to arrive at the foot of the hillside. Once the figure had caught up with Yusif, he introduced himself.

"Hi, my name is Amarik."

Amarik was now a lot lighter and brighter than when Yusif had first encountered him, sitting on the rock, at the edge of the forest.

"Pleased to meet you Amarik. My name is Yusif. How did you end up on the island?" Yusif asked him.

"I came here to check that the perimeter around the floating structures was still intact," said Amarik.

"I have been on the island for quite some time," Amarik said, "before you arrived, I was going to give up. I was mentally tired from the journey that had taken me to the edge of the forest," said Amarik.

Yusif nodded in agreement, as he too felt tired from the journey that had brought them to this point.

"I almost gave up a couple of times in the middle of the forest. This journey has pushed me almost to my limits," said Yusif, as he looked around to see if he could discover a way to get off this island, now that he believed his quest was over.

"Did you manage to pick up the rock crystal that was lying on the ground?" Amarik asked, as he adjusted his clothing from running.

"Yes, it took me a couple of attempts, but I managed to lift it and stand it upright," said Yusif.

"By the time I reached that crystal, I was too tired and did not have the strength. I tried to lift it, but I was unable to. I'm glad you managed to do it," said Amarik, as he turned around and sat down to rest on a nearby rock. "The only instructions I was given before I came to the island, was that I needed to follow the arrows. They would take me to the shimmering perimeter. It was my job to check it for any gaps," he explained to Yusif.

From where they were resting, they looked across the open space. In the far distance, they could see the swirling dark mass beginning to build up again. All the lost souls on the island were gathering at the edge of the forest. Yusif and Amarik quickly made their way towards the third large hillside, following the path that ran between the other two. All Yusif's senses told him there must be an opening somewhere close by. The fact that Amarik was trying to make his way to this point, was a good indication that he too, was looking for the same exit, which would allow them to leave this land. They started searching around the bushes at the base of the hill. After a while, Yusif came across a muddy mound of soft earth, covering both the surface of the hill and the ground nearby, so he started to dig with his hands and after a few moments, he found something.

"There's something under the surface of this hill and it's hard and smooth, not hilly material at all, this must be the way out," said Yusif, with an air of excitement in his voice.

He continued pulling at the soft mud, digging into the space he had made. Bits of overgrown undergrowth slid down from above, partially re-covering his excavation and making more work for Yusif. By the time he had pulled away the undergrowth, the tree spirits had indeed gathered into a large group at the edge of the forest. Amarik and Yusif could hear them, making noise and crying out, as if they had won a victory over them.

A long trail of dark energy made its way across the ground, from a smaller group, which was closer to Amarik and Yusif. It began to swirl around them as if caressing and stroking them. A foul smell made its way into their nostrils. Amarik began to darken as doubts flooded his mind. In that same moment, Yusif watched the mist as it swirled around himself. Haunting faces appeared in the fog, distracting his attention from pulling at the soft undergrowth and bushes. The faces were using fear to try and scare them. However, his determination and willpower were able to override his negative emotions, through which fear was trying to rise. Amarik and Yusif put their hands over their faces and held their breath, in a bid to stop the smell. Putting their hands down, they looked back and realised the small group was too far from the main body of dark fog, to do them any real harm.

Yusif could see that the main group was now moving towards them. It was like a large army, marching to war. As the large group got closer, he knew it was something he could not face by himself. He would have to join forces with Amarik to create a light force and send it in the direction of the army of darkness. There was nothing else Yusif could think of that could slow the marching army down. They stopped searching for the exit and turned around to face the tree spirit group.

"Focus, visualise a light coming from your body and radiating outwards as far as the group. This should force them to disperse or retreat," explained Yusif.

They stood there and watched as the army of darkness absorbed the energy force. They roared with delight, their faces filling with greed and excitement. Their eyes lit up, like the fiery embers of a furnace, as they glared in their direction. Their excitement caused a number of them to fall over one another. A group of them ended up in a pile on the floor where the light had struck them. This was not the kind of slowing down Yusif and Amarik had hoped for, but it gave them a little more time.

It became clear to Yusif and Amarik that what the tree spirits actually wanted, was the inner life force of the living, which was food for the tree spirits. Amarik and Yusif returned to frantically pull at the soft overgrown undergrowth, covering what they thought might be the exit they needed. As more of the soil covering the unknown structure within the hillside fell away, a flicker of light shone out from it, through the gap they had created with their digging.

"FASTER! FASTER!" shouted Yusif, as more of the undergrowth fell away to uncover the structure beneath it. They were both working as fast as they could.

"What is this?" Yusif asked out loud, as his digging had revealed there was a crystal structure behind the overgrown undergrowth. Yusif turned around and looked up at the hills around him and this was when he realised that they were not hills at all, but they were the crystal pyramids he had seen in the visions he had during his meditations.

"These are pyramids and not just hills covered with the undergrowth of the land," he said to Amarik.

They managed to clear a large space on the surface of the crystal structure, at least of person height. Yusif and Amarik watched as a beam of light shot out from the structure, directly to hit the red rock crystal. The rock crystal, absorbed the beam of light and as it did, it began to fill up with the light to shine brightly, no longer a dark colour, it was now lit with a beautiful red glow. They could see energy swirling around inside the red crystal as the beam of light from the crystal pyramid continued to feed it.

The most peculiar and unexpected thing happened next and Yusif was in awe of having witnessed it. A red beam of light shot out from the red rock crystal, which was in direct alignment with the rock crystal at the edge of the forest. As it shot out across the open space, it hit the army of tree spirits, splitting them into two groups, as it pierced their ranks. All the tree spirits came to a stop, looked at each other in confusion and then let out a massive roar.

"Yes!" Yusif whispered, as the light scattered the tree spirits. Amarik was a little more animated in his reaction.

"Alright! Take that!" Amarik yelled, as he jumped into the air with joy, punching his fist skyward.

The energy was a piercing light, which was too powerful for the tree spirits to absorb. Those who did try to absorb the light or were hit by it because they were standing in its trajectory, were burnt by its radiant beauty. The effect it had on them was like a fiery, piercing flame.

The light continued on its journey, hitting each of the remaining rock crystals in the circuit Yusif had activated and although Yusif couldn't see them all, as some were too distant, he knew instinctively that that was the case. For a moment, each of them started to glow and send out small pulses of energy. Suddenly and unexpectedly, the light source from the crystal pyramid extinguished, causing both Yusif and Amarik to turn away from the spectacle they were seeing, back to the crystal pyramid.

"Was that it?" Amarik asked.

"I'm not sure," replied Yusif.

They could see that the space in the hillside was now big enough for one person to get through. They both peered into it and could see it was a tunnel with a light at its opposite end. Yusif pushed Amarik through the opening and was amazed that he had disappeared from view.

Immediately after Amarik had disappeared into the tunnel, the beam of light from the crystal pyramid reactivated, again hitting the red rock crystal and re-energising it. The red rock crystal sent its beam of light onwards, through the open space, to the orange rock crystal and this time, the tree spirits moved aside instead of trying to block its path. As the beam of red light connected with the orange rock crystal, it lit up to glow a beautiful orange colour, however, in a change of behaviour from the initial pulse of energy originating from the crystal pyramid, the orange rock crystal sent out two beams of light, one red and the other orange. Both the red and orange beams of light struck the next and each of the rock crystals in turn and as they did, the other rock crystals pulsated much brighter than the first time they were re-energised and each rock crystal added their own colour to the beam, until all seven colours were contained within the beam of light. Even though Yusif could not physically see all of the rock crystals he had encountered since landing on the beach of the island, he received inspiration, knowing that all the rock crystals had been linked together by the crystal pyramid light and that from the green rock crystal, an additional beam of pink light energy shone forth. All eight colours reached out to the final rock crystal Yusif had hidden on the beach and it hungrily absorbed the energy it was being sent. The green rock crystal, which contained the pink light, was the first to send out a large pulse of energy, which travelled across the whole island, as though it was the pebble that had been dropped into a lake and from which its impact rippled out.

Yusif turned back to clamber through the entry way to the tunnel, he and Amarik had made earlier, however, the overgrowth from above had slid down and covered most of the space again, making it impossible for him to squeeze through and make his escape. Pulling the soil away from the entrance, he could sense the tree spirits were almost on him. From among the tree spirits, they sent out an extended arm that managed to wrap itself around Yusif's ankle. His ankle began to burn from the touch of this fog and as it began pulling Yusif towards the group, he grabbed hold of some bushes to try and stop himself being drawn towards the tree spirits. Unfortunately, the roots of the bushes were not established well enough or firmly in the soil and became uprooted, as he was pulled in the opposite direction. He tried scraping at the ground, in an effort to get some kind of hold. He also spun himself around onto his back, where he tried to sit up and pull the wrapped hold from around his ankle, which started to burn his already sensitive fingers. He also tried to stamp his foot into the ground to try and dislodge it, but nothing seemed to slow him down. He could do nothing to stop himself being pulled towards them. This was the first time he began to really panic during his journey to the island. He felt helpless to do anything to stop them getting to him, but that didn't stop him from trying.

Yusif's attempts to free himself from the tree spirit's grip had actually caused him and the 'arm' of their reach to change positions and he could see that they were moving closer to one of the beams of light that was now traversing the island. This gave Yusif an idea and so he started to roll over and over sideways, which was working to bring them even closer to the light beam. Eventually and to Yusif's relief, the out-stretched reach of the tree spirits crossed paths with the beam of light from the red rock crystal and it sliced through the dark energy and severed its grip on Yusif, causing that element of the tree spirit's energy to disperse into the atmosphere. Yusif was free. He didn't want to find out what would happen if he accidentally touched the beam of light, so he scrambled to his feet and ran to the cover of some rocks, where he could hide.

He looked across at the cavity in the cliff face. He knew that reaching it was his only hope of getting off the island, but he could not decide whether he should make a run for the pyramid and the space he had excavated, before it covered over completely or stay where he was. Looking out, over the rocks he had hidden behind, he could see the tree spirits closing in on him. He did not have too much time. It was now or never. He set off running for the pyramid, knowing he had scant few seconds to expand the entrance to a size big enough for him to fit through, so, once again, ignoring the pain, he tore at the soil frantically.

In the meantime, Earl felt a sudden urge to test out the crystal-singing bowl Mario had made. He had a special area where he liked to test out new instruments, so he carried the bowl to the balcony that overlooked the lake and valley. He carried it on a cushion that was made by someone in the city of Bakka, along with its special box that housed and protected the crystal wand he would use with the singing bowl. He placed them on the ledge of an open window before taking out the crystal wand and saying a short prayer. He attuned himself to the spiritual vibrations of energy that were all around him, placed the wand on the outer edge of the crystal bowl and started to move it around the top.

The crystal-singing bowl emitted a deep hum and with each

couple of cycles, the sound began to swell. Coloured lights appeared within the bowl, swirling around in time with the crystal wand movements causing the sound vibrations to increase. Earl started to fill with the same colours that were swirling around inside the bowl and he felt himself becoming one with the sound and light.

As the energy continued to build, Earl's consciousness began to transcend to a higher dimension of existence. Each of his seven spiritual bodies now existed in a different degree of consciousness. Each body was a replica of his spirit self in this dimension; each one turning a wand around a crystal bowl and radiating with a different coloured light, each generating a different musical note from the scale. The colours matched those of the crystal orbs he had gifted to Yusif for his quest. The energy vibrations and the colours from the seven singing bowls filled the room until they reached a pitch and resonance that drew each light from Earl's seven spiritual selves, sending them out into the atmosphere via the original singing bowl.

Unknown to both Earl and Yusif, but obviously with some divine intention, Earl's testing of the bowl was taking place and reaching its crescendo at the same time Yusif finally managed to clear away the overgrowth, which had covered the tunnel entrance to the crystal pyramid. Creating a larger opening, a red beam of light from the singing bowls, Earl was testing, came shining through the gap. With it came a beautiful loving sound and vibration of energy. This intensified beam of light struck the red rock crystal. The red glow of the rock crystal grew brighter and this was followed by an orange light, then yellow, green and so on, until all seven beams of light followed each other, reactivating the rock crystals of the same colour, causing each one to glow more brightly than ever before. There was a sudden intense pulse of energy from each of the rock crystals, which rippled across the island. With each pulse, a different musical note could be heard. The pulses threw the majority of the tree spirits all the way back to the edge of the forest, with the rest being scattered in every direction.

The next powerful pulse of energy from the rock crystals, froze the tree spirits in place, either where they were standing or where they had been scattered to and they each became spellbound. A bubble of energy wrapped around each of the tree spirits, causing them to become suspended, as if in rapture for a brief moment. Miraculously, from the ground where each of the tree spirits stood, roots started to grow, reaching up and connecting to the tree spirits, anchoring them so they could no longer move from their spot. Once the tree spirits were secured, tree bark began to form over them, travelling upwards from the ground, as they stood motionless. They screamed out and shook their branches in fear and confusion. Yusif could hear a lot of creaking and cracking, as the tree spirits shook their branches. A dark energy was released from each of the tree spirits, which spiralled up and formed into a giant, dark cloud, above them. The cloud began to circle around in the sky above and Yusif could see that faces appeared and disappeared within it. As it became more turbulent, thunder could be heard rumbling within it, followed by streaks of lightening, that flashed but did not seek to earth themselves on the ground. Yusif watched as a final flash streaked from one end to the other, causing the dark cloud to flicker, then fill with light. He could hear another rumble, as the cloud seemed to moan and groan with pain, circling the sky a few more times before it abruptly broke apart, dive bombing into the ground, where it was neutralised. The tree spirits settled down when they realised that something beautiful was happening to them. They were all turning back into trees, abundant with leaves and fruit, repaired from the devastation of the rock crystal landings.

Earl's spiritual bodies descended from the higher planes and joined together to become one body of light and love. Once he was fully back in his body, he stopped testing the crystal bowl and the beams of light produced by the singing bowl faded. As the light faded, the rock crystals stopped pulsing for a moment. Earl then packed up the crystal bowl, put the wand back in its box and carried them back to his studio.

A few seconds after the tree spirits had settled into their newly repaired homes and the crystal bowl had stopped singing, Yusif watched as the red rock crystal sent out a final pulse of energy. It moved through the atmosphere, spreading out across the whole island. This was followed by undulating ripples of energy, which left tiny water-like droplets behind them. Inside each droplet was the symbol shape that Earl had programmed into the small crystal orbs, Yusif had used earlier. The droplets filled the atmosphere over the island and hovered there, until the remaining rock crystals sent out their final pulses, adding more coloured droplets containing symbols, to the red ones already in the atmosphere and waiting. The droplets containing the Earthly signs then fell to the Earth, like a gentle shower of rain, quickly absorbed into the ground, giving life back to the island. All that was hibernating beneath the ground awoke and burst forth back into the light. It was now the end of the hibernation and the start of regrowth into renewal. The rest of the energy droplets fell onto the trees, rocks, water and some even created small patches of fire. The rest purified the air, creating gentle winds that freshened up the atmosphere. The symbols were that of Earth, Air, Fire, Water, Love, Change and Growth. All that the droplets touched, transformed that which they had landed on. Even Yusif felt a little energised, as the droplets fell on him.

All that had decayed on the island started to turn green. The rest of the tree spirits that were in hibernation began to awaken from their sleep. Fruit started to grow and ripen, leaves turned green or new shoots began to sprout from the branches of the trees. Soon the island was glowing with multiple colours of energy, as the new growth started to rapidly cascade. Yusif looked up to see that the sky was slowly beginning to clear. The land started to transform and become alive with vegetation. The tree spirits had transformed from darkness into light. They now had new homes and were finding peace within themselves. As the energy filled the island, all the trees bathed themselves, each of them sharing their inner love and light with those next to them. This helped them to heal and raised the vibrations of the whole island.

As the frequency and vibration around the island changed, it revealed the spiritual world that existed just beyond the decay of the island. The animals that existed within the spiritual dimension above the island's decay, began to appear again on the land. The animals had been waiting for this day to arrive, so that they could return to the island. When the darkness first came to the land, those that were enlightened managed to escape. They transcended to a higher vibration of energy. Here they remained, waiting for the land to return to a condition and vibration in which they could live and flourish once more. From the smallest to the largest of animals, they let their presence be known. Instead of a low vibrational humming, there was a calmness and a peace that filled the island. The sound of the birds and other animals living in the forest, brought the whole place to life. The transformation of the island was almost complete.

Back in Earl's studio, in the room with the giant singing bowls, the crystal wand circling the larger of the two, began to slow down its spin cycle. As one of the singing bowls slowed, so the other began to turn. The pitch in the room created by the singing bowls changed. The teleporter crystals transported the new sound to the forest and within the perimeter that encircled the floating rocks, the lower pitch was becoming a higher pitch, gently releasing the floating rocks and supporting them on their descent towards the ground, where they would settle. Some smaller pieces of rock broke away from the larger floating rocks, to settle in other places, their rightful places. In Earl's studio, both crystal wands were turning around the top of the bowl at the same speed. Once the floating rocks were back on the ground, the larger singing bowl slowed down to a stop. The wand over the smaller crystal bowl was now spinning faster. Its higher pitch started to shatter the rock that had become encrusted over the floating crystal structures. As it broke away from the crystal structure most of the encrusted rock turned to dust and was blown away by a breeze. Once all the crusting had fallen away, all that was left was the beautiful, shining, crystal structures. The spinning wand slowed down to a stop once the structure was back on the ground. The shimmer in the forest that had surrounded the floating rocks began to fade until it disappeared altogether.

Now that the once ravaged land had recovered from the decay, Yusif cautiously made his way over to the newly transformed trees. As he approached them, their faces appeared from the trunks. They thanked God for sending someone to help restore the land. They spoke to Yusif about the completion of the task that allowed them to transform back into beautiful healthy trees again.

"All we ever wanted was to transform back into how we were before the decay came to the land," said the tree spirit, as its newly formed branches swayed in the breeze.

"Your appearance and approach made those who came to help, fear you," said Yusif.

"Yes, we understand this now, but we were driven on by a ravenous need to transform ourselves back to how we were. We were overwhelmed by our immediate needs, even though within us remained an awareness of choice. We lost the belief in the choices that came to us as inspiration. We thought we knew best. We thought our way was the easiest and quickest solution to our problems. Instead of being patient and seeking the grace of God and a peaceful solution, we became of those who push and shove things around. We now see with a clear vision, that patience and a belief in God, would have been the better choices. We became the attackers of the innocent. We were filled with a desperate need that drove us to have an aggressive approach towards anyone we saw. When we detected a soul's inner light, we tried to steal it, in a bid to transform ourselves. May God have mercy on our souls."

As they were talking, Yusif realised that the reason for everything he had learnt while in Bakka, was about seeing beyond what was in front of him. The end result revealed the greater divine plan at work. When he was in the middle of the forest, even he could not have imagined such a beautiful outcome. He did feel sorry for the tree spirits. He looked out over the land and noticed how quickly things had changed and transformed. That was when it really came home to him that God, is indeed, the master planner. He surrounds all and is always the additional person, at every event and meeting, as things are planned and discussed. It is His plan that is playing out and not the plan made by others. Yusif thanked God for allowing him enough wisdom and strength to play his part. His striving to trust and listen to the best of his thoughts, helped him to complete the task. Without the inspiration from God, Yusif knew within himself, that he would have become lost to the darkness. His approach would have been different to the one God had designed for him to follow. He thanked God again, for the help that allowed him to strive and better himself. The whole experience helped him to grow in understanding, for the benefit of his own soul. At the same time, he was sorry for the doubts that filled his mind. Now his task was complete, as he reflected, he realised that there was just enough help to keep him focused and striving. If there had been too much help, then he would have handed the task over to those in the higher Heavens and he would have sat back and been of those who do nothing. He was grateful that the task had been entrusted to him.

Yusif was thoughtful and quiet for a time while he remembered that striving allows each of us to reach our highest and greatest potential; to reach out beyond the thoughts that are manifesting about our immediate situation. He realised that because we think it, it does not make it the only reality, there is always a reality that we cannot see. It is we who must strive, to bring about the change, to create a new reality. His conclusion was that his striving, commitment and a belief in the truth and trust, helped him to complete the task. Those who are striving, are the real change for good and peace on Earth. Behind all Yusif did, God was directing, sustaining, influencing and inspiring him, to perfect himself.

"There is a lot of encouragement to help us strive to complete the tasks that are given to us. We too were striving, in our own way. What has happened, here today, has been a lesson in surrendering to the love, trust and truth within," said the tree spirit.

Once the conversation had finished, Yusif turned around and made his way back across the open space. What was once a barren place, was now green with grass. The overgrowth had slid off the pyramids and before him, they stood radiantly in the beautiful sunlight. As he walked up the track between them, he noticed that where the red rock crystal had stood, was nothing more than a pile of dust, most of which had been blown away. The same thing had happened to the other six rock crystals into which Yusif had placed one of Earl's small crystal orbs. By the time he reached the pyramid with the tunnel, through which Amarik had crawled, he was beginning to feel a little happier.

He stood in front of it and looked up. He contemplated going up the stairs to have a look inside but changed his mind. He decided to go through the same exit as Amarik. He'd had enough excitement for the time being and the need to get back to the beach, was his main thought. Crawling through the tunnel, he found himself in a cavern. At its centre was a circular hole, with a teleporter crystal floating in the middle, about halfway down. Like Yusif did the first time he came across such a circular hole, he sat on the edge, gradually pushed himself off and floated down towards the teleportation crystal, which transported him to a place filled with light.

It took a moment for his eyes to adjust to this light and as soon as they did, he looked around to see if he could find Amarik, but soon realised he was alone again. He started walking and sending out thoughts to his companions, when he suddenly remembered about the rock crystal that he had left on the island's beach. Now back in the light, his inner vision returned and in his mind's eye he saw the rock crystal on the beach. He could see the crystal had now grown and was filled with colours that swirled around inside. He was relieved, because he had forgotten about the crystal he'd left, with all that had taken place on the island, during the last part of the quest.

Back on the Beach

The companions that had taken Yusif to the island, returned and he now felt safe and protected. His exhaustion from the flight away from tree spirits and the battle he had, to free himself of their grip, both, made Yusif succumb to his tiredness and he collapsed to the ground in relief and soon fell fast asleep.

He awoke to find himself back on the beach of Bakka. He sat up and noticed that there was a circle of individual crystals surrounding his prone body. He felt reinvigorated, his wounds had been healed, his energy balanced and his garments restored; he took a deep breath and stretched his hands up to the sky, letting himself fall back to the ground. He was now lying on his back looking up at the sky. He felt happy to be alive and back on the beach.

Yusif noticed a number of footprints in the sand. It was as if others had stood over him while he lay there. One set of footprints headed off in the direction of the crystal on the far side of the beach, another set could be seen in the direction of the crystal cave and the city of Bakka and yet another, headed back up the pathway that had brought him to the beach.

Standing up, Yusif made his way to the stack of crystals through which the Crilarian had first spoken to him. The faces of the Crilarian appeared. This time various faces came through all at the same time. They wanted to hear what he had to say about his journey. They completely surrounded the stack of crystals so nothing of the stack could be seen. He explained to them, telling them of his adventure. One of the faces spoke on behalf of the group soul.

"We are pleased to see you again. We will soon know if the task was completed. Our praise and glory first goes out to God. If His vision did not encompass all, guide each of us in turn, all hope would be lost. He gives each soul an opportunity to grow and develop and reach out beyond their station," said the Crilarian, as all the faces that surrounded the rock crystal nodded and chatted among themselves in agreement.

"The task was definitely taxing on the inner self. The words of encouragement you shared with me, played a part in my being able to complete the task. They help shape my perception and they strengthened me in moments of weakness. I thank you for sharing your thoughts of wisdom," said Yusif, as he smiled and expressed gratitude and appreciation.

"We only speak as directed by the spirit of inspiration. Thank you," said the Crilarian, with the rest of them saying, "thank you," in unison.

The Crilarians smiled and all the faces faded away. Yusif turned to look over the lake at the rainbow surrounding the structure. A form rose out of the lake. It was one of the Zamureons. The Zamureon was able to manipulate the water around itself so that it could speak.

"You did all you were meant to do, no more and no less. All that is asked of anyone is that they do their best. This is what God asks of us and so this is what we ask of each other. Those who follow the signs that are revealed to them, benefit the most, as they develop and maintain their good character," said the Zamureon.

"I wish I had not doubted as much as I did during the quest. I feel that if I had believed more, I would not have made such judgements in the face of, what I thought was, a dangerous situation. As the doubts arose, I opened the door to the irregularities within. They clouded the purpose and true vision of the quest at times," admitted Yusif to the Zamureon.

"All actions that manifest are a part of the grand plan. It is good that you can see where you could make improvements in the development of yourself. What you learn about yourself is as valuable as the task itself. Both play a part in the game of life. One benefits you, the other benefits all. The vision of an evolved soul is that there is no good or bad, however, there is personal growth and development. It is not for an evolved soul to judge any actions but to express love and follow the best of their thoughts; to believe and trust in the divine plan at work," replied the Zamureon.

"I will try better next time," Yusif asserted.

"We must each learn and expand our horizons. Strive to see beyond the limitations that surround you. God will send to you what you are capable of understanding and accepting as truth. If you reject something because you do not want to accept it is true, you slow down your growth and development. Your acceptance of wisdom raises your consciousness to the Heaven, where your vision sees more. Those that reach out will receive inspiration and divine guidance," continued the Zamureon.

Yusif smiled again as he understood, accepted and related what was said, to his misconception about his journey to the island. The Zamureon submerged back into the water.

There was one place Yusif had not yet been, since he arrived in this world and learnt about its existence. He walked over to the beautiful rock crystal on the beach, joined by his companions, who he still did not know much about. He could feel a beautiful energy being released from the rock crystal, he was mesmerised by it and could not take his eyes off it, as radiant colours swirled around inside it. One particular colour interested Him, as he had never seen a colour like it before.

"This colour has been specially created. As it matures, it will change and expand in both vibration and colour. The energy behind the colour, will become accessible to those who strive to raise their consciousness. Earl was instrumental in developing and bringing this sacred vibration from the higher Heavens," said the companion.

"What will the colour and its vibration be used for?" Yusif asked, as he continued to watch the colour swirl around within the crystal.

"It will become a new light within the Heavens where souls are able to reside. As souls ascend, they will draw from this energy. The wisdom contained within the new light will help them break down the old belief systems that have been established by the irregularities. As this wisdom becomes established on Earth, there will be a return to the truth. Energy creates vibrations, vibrations create sound, sound creates colour. This colour contains a sacred symbol that will be a part of the new changes on Earth. As the colour assimilates itself into the human psyche, those who strive, will receive inspiration about the pathway that will allow their consciousness to ascend. Those in the darkness, will fear and ridicule the new ideas that are revealed to those who reach out. This is because they have built their foundations on certain Earthly comforts. To maintain those comforts, they rely on the creation of a certain human condition on Earth. Many of the Earthly conditions only serve the self and Earthly comforts are nothing, compared to the comforts and splendour of the hereafter. Free from the Earthly conditions, the human soul is able to flourish. As those who are awake strive to open their awareness, they realise that they do not need many of the things created out of the Earthly material. They will become more aware of the journey through the light and the life of the hereafter. They will begin to realise what qualities they need to develop and grow to make the journey home. They will begin to turn inwardly towards their true centres and seek that which benefits their soul and rely more on a foundation of piety and love.

"The new energy will help many to see beyond the created conditions that bind many to the life of the world. They will begin to recognise that all they really need, is within. Those who are ready, will use this energy to help in the spiritual advancement of humanity. Through their springs in the Earth, this new colour will show up in their aura. Those who are working with this energy will share their understanding with their children. What they pass on will allow their children to gain access to the essence of this energy. They will use it to develop and enhance their spiritual awareness. They will bridge the gap between the Earth plane and the hereafter. The springs in the Earth will change, allowing those who expand their awareness to hold and express greater spiritual truths from the higher dimensions," said one of the females, from his group of companions.

As Yusif walked around the rock crystal, he was drawn to a lone crystal lying in the sand. He picked it up and to his surprise, it glowed brightly in his hands and he could feel its energy running through him. He instantly knew that his rock crystal was assigned to him, as it spoke to him in a personal way.

Yusif sat down to study the crystal some more and was amazed when an image appeared in its faceted centre. He watched the first image avidly and then he realised that he could flick through the different events it had stored, like flicking through the chapters of a *Kindle* book. He came across a couple of images that surprised him. He saw the island that he had visited, where on the beach, a lone figure opened a bag and took out a rock crystal. He placed it on the sandy beach and made his way towards the embankment. As he reached the top of the embankment, he saw the violet-coloured rock crystal, sitting there, at the top. He watched as the crystal was cleaned and a crystal orb of the same colour was merged into it, creating a pulse of energy and generating a message in the form of an arrow made of sticks. He then looked around to see if he could see anyone else. Yusif could hear the thoughts that manifest around the figure in the crystal.

"If someone else sees the arrow, they will know in which direction I have walked," thought the lone figure, Yusif was watching in the crystal.

He watched more of the images and became convinced that he was the character in the images, as it mimicked his own journey he had just been on to complete his quest. However, this telling or recollection, stored in the crystal, ended right after he had travelled to the edge of the desert, recording his decision not to follow the other pathway that led to the forest. It showed how he had become confused about where he was and how he was feeling drained of energy and could go no further. It showed him sitting down to rest for a while, but he actually fell asleep and had to be rescued from the island by his companions, eventually waking to find himself back on the beach of the beautiful island. Yusif could not shake off the feeling that he was the character in the image. *But how could this be?* He could not remember ever having visited this island before. His companions smiled and nodded their heads a couple of times without saying a word. They then left Yusif to make up his own mind about what he was actually seeing.

Yusif flicked to the next chapter. Again, he saw himself back on the deserted island. He repeated all the steps from the previous chapter but managed to make it as far as the forest, this time, having changed his mind about entering the desert. It showed him finding the indigo rock crystal and repeating the necessary steps to activate the pulse, but as he left, to follow the arrow, he unfortunately became lost. Inexplicably, he must have fallen asleep again, waking to find himself back on the beach again.

He flicked forward to another lifetime. Again, he saw himself on the island for a third time. Taking the track to the forest, he reached a blue rock crystal, this time. He saw the arrow he was meant to follow, but the next memory was of him waking on the beach once again. On the island for the fourth time, he reached the green rock crystal that had fallen over, he struggled to lift and stand it upright. In the end he left it on the ground where it was, with no recollection recorded of how he ended up back on the beach again. Flicking again he reached the yellow rock crystal. Moving on he reached the orange rock crystal at the edge of the forest. He counted six. He noted that each time he visited the island, he reached one more rock crystal and followed one more arrow to show the direction he had to travel. He did not have the strength to make it across the open desert. He tried but was attacked by the mist that surrounded him. He retreated back into the woods where he felt safe. Again, he fell asleep and for the sixth time and woke to find himself back on the beach.

He continued to review things that he had obviously previously recorded and was amazed to see how in-depth the memories were. Every moment of his whole existence was there, recorded in his soul stone. Every thought, word and deed in full colour. He continued to look at various times he had visited Earth. This also made him aware that you can have many different Earthly parents, over many lifetimes. In many of the lifetimes, he was joined by a mysterious female energy. It was as if their lives were interlocked. He began to wonder why he had not met her in his present life. Then he noticed that now and again, there were gaps when she would act as a guide and inspiration from the hereafter, as he went through some of his worldly experiences unaccompanied. He too would act as her guide and inspiration from the hereafter, during some of her lifetimes.

Although some lifetimes were spent alone, their spiritual benefits were plentiful. Now that he had had a chance to see his life like this, he understood that, maybe, this life was one of those lifetimes in which he had to make the journey unaccompanied. As he pondered the idea, he continued to watch details about his many lives. He grew in understanding as he watched his lives in this way. Yusif could see how each lifetime allowed him to grow in love. He could now understand and see how some of his many mistakes had been the fuel for his greatest achievements later on. He watched as the dark energy he created became the base matter into which he was reborn. He also understood how to truly strive in the way of God. The real *hajj* was to strive and reach the home of the hereafter. It was through meditation that his striving allowed him to rise above the darkness and into the light.

He skipped to the end hoping to see something of his future. He laughed to himself, as he got to the end and saw a reflection of himself in the crystal. He could see the present moment and was not permitted to see beyond that. He knew that the future was known; that all things which manifest on Earth are predestined and in place, two days before the event takes place in the physical world. He believed you can influence the future of the human race through the choices you each make. Yusif looked at his friends with an enquiring gaze, but they just smiled. When he realised they were not going to tell him what he wanted to know, in relation to the female in the café, he sighed. He decided to put the crystal back where he picked it up. Yusif stood up and was about to put the crystal back where he found it, when his companions beckoned him to wait a moment. They told

Yusif to stretch out his hand and hold the crystal in the direction of the large crystal in front of him. As he did, a beam of light extended from the larger crystal to the crystal in his hand. He could see many of the images recorded from his past disappearing. These images were his mistakes, regrets, pain, guilt and unhappiness that he had manifested during his lifetimes. His companions told him that those moments of uncertainty had now been replaced with a loving energy. God forgives repeatedly and removes the stains from the record of deeds as He pleases. This paved the way for a smoother journey, the next time he cycled through life.

The larger crystal began to glow, sending out little pulses of energy like the kind Yusif experienced on the island during its transformation. Yusif moved his crystal closer and as the two touched, the smaller one in his hand was absorbed into the larger one in front of him. After a short while, his crystal re-emerged and Yusif took the crystal and held it in his hand. He sat back down and meditated while holding the crystal, which allowed him to integrate into his spiritual self, the new energy frequencies held within the crystal. It was a beautiful experience. This joining was an initiation into the beginning of yet another stage of his spiritual journey. As the large crystal in front of him returned to its original glow, Yusif awakened from his meditation. He left the crystal where he found it, as he knew if he needed it, he would be drawn to wherever it was.

Standing up, Yusif looked into the larger crystal that came from the higher Heavens. There came into view a picture of the whole Earth. It was as if he was looking at the world from a great distance. It was inspired to Yusif that preparations were well under way for the return of many souls. They would be born into physical bodies to help in the healing and transformation of the Earth and its inhabitants. They would carry within them this new colour as a little spark of light. Those who remained true to themselves would reach out beyond that which exists for many, as a worldly reality. Using the wisdom that flows from the heavenly heights, they would eventually be admitted to dwell within this heavenly light.

"Those who meditate and strive will be drawn up in stages and contractions. They will share what they receive as inspired wisdom," said one of his companions.

The vision in the crystal skipped forward to a future time of life on Earth, where Yusif saw a bright light, descending to land on the Earth. There was a sudden burst of light from where this soul had landed, which radiated out to encircle the whole planet. Yusif looked at his companions with a smile and returned to watching the images in the crystal. A close-up image appeared and Yusif could see the outline of a man standing at the top of a short flight of stairs of about ten steps. In the background, behind this figure, were two pillars with an arched window that was filled in with stone. On the ground where he stood was a square paving stone, with an image etched into it, making it different from the others around it. There were also ten of his close companions standing next to him, five on either side. No one stood on the steps. At the bottom of the steps, there were two rows of people facing each other; each row was three deep and they made two lines half the length of the square courtyard enclosure, in which they were all standing. Yusif watched himself join those that had gathered. He understood instinctively that those in the world who were enlightened enough, during their time on Earth, would see his face, it would appear to them in their mind's eye. A little beyond this enclosure was the place where the final battle between the forces of light and darkness would take place on Earth.

The light that Yusif saw in the rock crystal was the return of Isa (Jesus). The image gradually faded and Yusif was left looking into a clear rock crystal.

Once the image faded, they all stepped away from the crystal. A beam of light from this rock crystal shot out in the direction of the island that Yusif had visited, lighting up the rock crystal that Yusif had left on the island's beach. Each of the seven colours in the crystal on the island became fully energised and they swirled around inside it. Once the rock crystal on the beach had been fully activated, the crystal in front of Yusif and his companions, sent out a second beam of light, heading to the crystal structure on the lake. At the same time, a beam of light also went out from the rock crystal Yusif had left on the beach. Both lights met above the tray slab of crystal that was fastened to the central pillar on top of the structure, where there simultaneously manifested a large crystal. All three crystals were now connected and they were radiating and sending out pulses of energy in every direction.

A beautiful vibration of energy went out from the crystal on top of the structure on the lake. It could be seen moving through the atmosphere. A ripple vibrating energy completely filled this dimension. You could see the energy of the pulse rise high above the land. As it moved through the atmosphere, it radiated the seven different colours of the rainbow as well as the new colour, which seemed to stay in the sky for a while. It was there for long enough for all to see, and then faded away, leaving only a small trace of itself.

In the library where Yusif met Khadija, new book categories started to appear on the shelves' label holders. This was where Yusif's hand had passed through the books, when he tried to pick one to read. The books also started to manifest in a way that would allow those visiting the library to take them from the shelves and read them. The books would be available to those who were going to visit Earth. Some of the books contained information about how to work with this new energy. Mario was sent inspiration to start working on new crystals that would hold this new energy. Those who were enlightened would be able to tap into this new colour, retrieve the information, and share it with those they met in the Earth plane. To reach this sacred inner knowledge, they would have to meditate and strive to enter their inner sacred mosque. This sacred knowledge was out of reach of those who did not look within themselves. Only those who turn towards their true centre would find this knowledge and understand its relevance in the world. This information spoke of a pathway, a journey that takes them to this new land, in the higher Heavens. This new dimension would become the home of any who are willing to reach out with love.

The heavenly station in which they were residing received a blessing from God. The long-awaited manifestation of the crystal, leading to the activation and transformation of Bakka, was set in motion. Everything became transformed by a spiritual degree. The energy from the three crystals subsided. Unlike the ones on the island that turned to a fine dust, these crystals remained where they were. The restored island Yusif had visited, would become the home to the new souls waiting to ascend to this new station.

Yusif was shown in his mind's eye, the top of the new structures on the island. He pondered for a moment as he saw what looked like a flat tray on top of one of the crystal structures.

Where is the crystal? What was inside the pyramids on the island? He thought to himself. Yusif had always been fascinated by the pyramids on Earth and he was disappointed that he did not have time to explore the inside of the pyramids, while he was on the island.

Maybe next time, he thought to himself.

Yusif looked up at his companions, who simply nodded at him, knowing, just as Yusif did, that it was time to go, even though Yusif did not want to leave, the companions moved closer to him and told him he had work to do elsewhere. Trying to prolong the stay, Yusif quizzed the companions about the footprints he had seen in the sand, but they were tight lipped about that, however, they did tell Yusif that he would meet Amarik again, who would invite him to his wedding. They suggested he attend because there would be someone he needed to meet; someone who would help him with another task in the future. So, he reluctantly walked with them from the beach to the footpath.

"You have completed this stage in your learning. Follow the guidance that comes from the spirit of inspiration. This will lead to right actions. Remain true to yourself and you will continue to grow," said one of the companions.

The companion explained that the new garments, with radiating ornaments Yusif had acquired, would expand his conscious awareness. They would allow him to continue communicating and working with those in the hereafter. He would in time, gain access to higher states of conscious awareness; that he would be able to see and connect with the spiritual world, with greater clarity during his physical life. As they passed the fields on their way back up the hillside, Yusif paused to take one last look at the valley. The flowers in the fields swayed in the breeze, their fragrance enchanting the atmosphere. Earl's music continued to fill the land. These sights and sounds would remain with him forever.

His newfound friends embraced him and they set off on the final return journey. They reached the top of the hillside, entering into a patch of clouds, the air brisk but invigorating and when Yusif turned back to speak with the companions, they had disappeared. Yusif took his next step and found himself standing beside his physical body, in his meditation room, back on Earth. He paused for a moment, looking around the room, then stepped forward and sat down in the position of his body. It was strange; he could feel the heavy, wet, weight of his physical body. Once his consciousness had fully returned, he took a deep breath, his physical chest expanding, rising and falling with each breath. The four companions that had been his guides, surrounded him.

"You were never alone for a moment and you never will be," said one of the female companions.

To his surprise, another spirit being joined the group. Yusif instantly recognised him as his grandfather. They did not exchange any words, they did not have to. The love and respect they had for each other was enough to replace anything they might have said.

One of the female companions stepped forward to remind Yusif to tell others that their world was but a loving thought away.

"All it takes is a kind heart and a perception of unconditional love that embraces all. Love and its expression will raise your soul's vibrations and expand your consciousness. For those who choose love, over the irregularities, will prosper. They will become a dweller in the lands on high. Your real home is where your consciousness resides. No irregularities can enter the greater heavenly states of awareness. We are ever around each of you, inspiring you with guidance. We hear all your thoughts and prayers and respond to those that come to us in love, truth and trust," said another of the companions. She then blew in Yusif's direction and he could smell the freshness of the valley on her breath. Their parting words to him were:

"**As Salamu Alaikum**, rest now my brother, we will soon return."

"**Wa alaikum as-salam**," replied Yusif.

Yusif knew that everyone was in safe hands, as the curtain to the hereafter was drawn. As his companions slowly disappeared, he was left looking at the blank wall in his dimly lit room.

Yusif sat there for a few moments, getting used to the feel of a heavy body again. He stretched, wiped his face with his hands and leaned over to pour himself a drink of water from the jug on the table. He stood up and went downstairs into the kitchen to boil some water and as he waited for it to boil, he retrieved the letter from behind the cupboard in the other room. He made his way to the living room, opening the letter as he went, but pausing in the hallway and reflecting over the contents, when the doorbell rang unexpectedly. He flinched in surprise and rushed to answer the door, in his haste, knocking over a small table with a book on it. Straightening himself up and righting the table, he took a deep breath to prepare himself, feeling embarrassed he had been so jumpy. Shaking his head at himself, he opened the door.

He was met by the sound of a female voice. She expressed an apology for disturbing him and introduced herself as a friend of the next-door neighbour, reaching out to shake his hand. Yusif was immediately intrigued, although he tried not to show it, when he spotted a beautifully crafted, silver bracelet, embedded with thirteen different coloured gemstones, around her wrist. Yusif told her about the phone call from his neighbour to say that they were stuck in traffic. He explained that during the earlier conversation with Alisha, the phone cut off and he had not heard from her since. While this conversation was taking place, Yusif could not help but to remember the incident in the café and the exact same bracelet that had fallen on the floor.

"You are welcome to try calling her from my house phone," Yusif suggested.

"I have been trying to contact her, but the phone is going straight to the answer machine. They have not responded to my message yet," said the woman, her worry palpable.

"You are welcome to wait here until they arrive home," he offered, as he opened the door wider.

The only visible sign of how he was feeling, was the smile on his face, which was matched by the stranger. She played with her hair then flicked it back and stepped forward entering his home. Deep down, Yusif recalled how he'd felt back in the café, during his first encounter with her; that of being immediately overwhelmed by the instantaneous recognition of a deep love, which connected him to this female. This, he realised, was the very moment he had been waiting for, for much of his adult life. And yet, he still did not know her name! He also remembered what Sara had said to him, "'Ah yes, a soul's consciousness can travel ahead of time. It is part of the connections that are made between people. Most people are unaware of these connections that are made in advance....'"

Perhaps Yusif and his new acquaintance will have their own adventures in the future, but that's another story, for another time.

THANK YOU ALL so very much for going on this enlightening adventure with Yusif, I hope you enjoyed reading it as much as I enjoyed writing it! I also hope that the spiritual experiences Yusif encountered, have inspired you to take into your own hearts love, truth and trust, with the knowledge that enlightenment, closeness to God, peace and spirituality will aid you in the learning of lessons, through reflection, thinking and contemplating on the signs of God, scattered across the world

Additional Reading

Self-Help Guide To Meditation And The Quran
Available on Amazon
By
Asif Saba

Reincarnation and The Quran
Available on Amazon
By
Asif Saba

Printed in the United States
by Baker & Taylor Publisher Services